Silence Golden

Contemporary Kink-Inspired Erotica

Edited by
Anna Sky

A
Sexy Little Pages
Publication

For more great erotica, visit www.SexyLittlePages.com/books

ISBN 978-1-5333730-3-8

CONTENTS

A CHANGE OF PERSPECTIVE
by Annabeth Leong

I had stepped into someone else's life. Everything I had on was new or rented—the tuxedo, the shining black leather shoes, the binder that concealed my breasts, the cock stuffed into the front of my pants.

The woman on the other end of the leash I was holding didn't belong to me either. Kristina, my best friend, had begged me to put on this show for just one night, for just this party, and I had agreed.

I had stripped her naked, buckled her into a leather collar so thick she couldn't bend her neck, locked it with the padlock she had given me, and led her into the main party room by a leash handle that could double as a spanking implement. The temptation was to clutch it because I wasn't sure I knew what I was doing, but I forced myself to hold it loosely instead. Max, the character I was playing tonight, wasn't the type to over-grip. He was the definition of cool and smooth, because I'd made him up to be that way, and I focused on walking and moving like I'd imagined he would.

Because of nerves, we'd arrived a little late. Kristina

hadn't been to any kinky events since she'd broken up with her ex, and we'd had a long talk about that before getting dressed. I went out like this most weekends, but not usually as a top, and never presenting as a man. I'd spent forever in the bathroom adjusting the package I'd purchased for the occasion, half-worried I hadn't put it on right and half-overwhelmed by how turned on I got seeing its bulge.

The party was already in full swing. The seemingly required soundtrack of Massive Attack and Hybrid pumped steadily through high-quality speakers, ordinary household objects were hidden under black cloths, and kink furniture had been brought out and set up throughout the space. The carpet must have been steam cleaned earlier that day—a slightly damp, soapy smell wafted through the air-conditioned room.

I'd been going to private kinky parties for years, but the first moment inside I always felt like I was in the wrong place. I never could sort out the details of the press of bodies, and the sounds of gasps, moans, grunts, and screams hit me with a sense of danger that took a few minutes to transform into a vicarious thrill. Usually, that was when I would lean toward the person I came with, wrap myself in their toppy energy, and let our power dynamic settle my nerves.

Tonight, I was the top. The chain that linked me to Kristina stirred. She shifted from foot to foot like a nervous animal, and I knew what she needed because it was what I would have needed in her position.

I picked up the slack in the chain until it stretched taut. Choking up to keep her on a short leash, I steered us toward a spot deeper in the party as if I knew exactly where we were going. I didn't, but she didn't have to know that.

I could feel her calming with every step. She followed me like a dancer, up on her tiptoes because I had a few inches on her, her bare feet landing precisely, the movements making the muscles in her thick calves and thighs flex and ripple. I thought it was a beautiful effect, so I shifted my grip to urge her higher onto her toes.

Her posture changed even more. Her straight neck translated to a straight back. We'd decided not to use any restraints besides the collar and lead, but she moved her hands into position behind her as if I'd cuffed them there, and the gesture emphasized the curves of her breasts, stomach, and hips.

Her thick, curly hair cascaded down her back, tendrils brushing the tops of her thumbs. She kept her eyes lowered, which made the beauty of her long lashes more noticeable and made me feel safe watching her face.

I wasn't used to looking at my best friend this way. Of course, I knew she was pretty, but I didn't usually admire the sensual fullness of her cheeks. I'd never before stared at the spot below her ear and thought about putting my tongue there. I'd certainly never mentally compared the coppery brown of her lips and her nipples, had never wondered if the latter were hardening because of me.

I'll admit, I'd forgotten the role I was supposed to be playing. A bottom might get to go la-la in subspace, but a top can't give in to the temptation to neglect the rest of the world.

I was so focused on Kristina that I walked into a tall someone's chest. In my surprise, I jerked the leash to an odd angle, making her stumble.

I opened my mouth to apologize to both of them, then remembered who I was tonight and closed it. I didn't know how well I passed to other people, but I passed great to myself as long as I didn't say anything. I felt like Max, felt like a handsome, sexy, well-put-together, dominant man—right up until the soprano tones of my voice hit my eardrums. I'd experimented with lowering it, but that just made me feel ridiculous. Instead, Kristina and I had agreed that Max would be the strong, silent type. We'd even worked out signals I could use to check in with her, so I wouldn't have to break the spell while we were in front of other people at the party.

We hadn't anticipated a situation where I'd need to communicate with anyone but her.

"Hey man, are you going to just stand there?" the guy said.

I allowed myself a momentary flush of pleasure. If I weren't passing, he wouldn't have addressed me with hey man. He needed something, though. I tugged Kristina closer, bringing her to stand closer at my side, and gestured toward the man, hoping she would understand that I wanted her to handle the interaction.

Kristina dipped her chin as far as her collar allowed and dropped to her knees. "Please forgive the mistake," she said. We'd first met in a drama class at the local community theater, and she'd learned a lot since then. Even from her position on the floor, Kristina had no trouble making herself heard over the party's trip-hop soundtrack. The woman knew how to project.

"Please accept my apologies on behalf of myself and my master," she continued. "It was my fault he bumped into you—I was... distracting him."

Her words sent an unexpected flush of heat through my body. Apparently, she knew I'd been looking at her. Apparently, she'd been playing herself up for me.

I forced my awareness back to the guy in front of us, but he was all haze to me. My eyes were on his strong jaw and brawny build, but all I saw in my mind was the top of Kristina's head, her curly hair spreading out in all directions, and the smooth, dark skin of her breasts jutting out below.

"Tell your master he's a lucky man," the guy said with a snort. "No big deal. I'd be distracted, too."

His leer did get my attention, and that set off a different sort of heat—a tight squeezing in my chest that told me I was taking this evening a little too seriously.

I dropped my hand to the top of Kristina's head, instinctually reaching for my partner to ground myself. I remembered a second too late that she wasn't actually my partner—we hadn't negotiated any sexual play between us, just that I'd take her out and lead her around on the leash.

She pressed up into my hand, though, her body language very like that of a purring cat. I couldn't resist stepping closer, and Kristina shifted so the whole naked length of her was warm against my clothed legs.

My fingers tightened on the leash. All this was going to my head. That chain and collar sent so many signals that she was mine. Seeing her on her knees, feeling her cuddle up against me, hearing her refer to me as her master—all those things gave me the same intoxicating impression. I didn't top often, but I knew the hot, feral feelings I got when I did. I knew the swagger, the rush of power, the jolt of arousal that shot in to fill the space created by someone else's surrender.

I petted my best friend's head, right there in the middle of the party. Various desires rushed into my mind, jumbled but urgent.

I knew I ought to talk to her. I didn't want to pull us out of here, though. This thing I was feeling seemed like an effect of the party and the situation itself. If we went out to the kitchen and the room where people could change, if I went back to my ordinary coat, and if I heard my ordinary voice, then I was pretty sure I'd lose the magic of this moment, of being Max, of being someone who could be Kristina's master.

I tugged her gently to her feet. Her eyes were wide and unfocused and she looked well on her way to subspace. Mentally, I cursed. I was so tempted to take advantage of the opportunities that were appearing in front of us, but I didn't want to abuse the circumstances or my best friend's trust. I didn't want to start doing things to her when she was in a vulnerable, quiescent state.

I made the okay sign with my hand, my thumb and first finger forming a circle, and my other fingers lifted. We'd agreed on that as a check-in gesture.

Kristina nodded enthusiastically. "Very okay." Her cheeks were flushed. She leaned against me, and now I felt the heat of her through the layers of my tuxedo jacket and white shirt and binder. How was her naked body so warm, so able to touch me the way that counted even through so much clothing? I inhaled to steady myself, but the effort backfired because I caught a strong whiff of Kristina—not only her coconut-scented shampoo and the lime of her body lotion, but beneath that, the oceanic scent of her arousal. I could have drowned in that.

I made the sign again. Kristina laughed. "Are you okay?" Her eyes sharpened as she studied me.

That was better. She seemed less foggy now. If she was checking me for damage, that meant she'd engaged her critical thinking skills and I could trust her to actually use her judgment.

I nodded, and then guided us out of the main walkway, finding us space against a wall. How to communicate what I wanted from her? I didn't want to get too toppy just yet because that would risk throwing her back into subspace, so I deliberately didn't recreate the image in my mind, the one where I used the leash to position her with her back to the wall exactly the way I wanted. That sort of dominance could come later, if she agreed to what I hoped to silently propose.

Instead, I left the leash slack and put my hand to her cheek. Keeping my gaze locked with hers, I allowed the touch to turn sensual. I traced down to the line of her jaw. She inhaled sharply but didn't move. I stroked that spot below her ear that I'd been looking at before. Her lips parted, and I ran the pad of my thumb over her lower one. Then I asked again with the hand gesture. Okay?

She nodded, but then her forehead wrinkled. I made a rolling gesture with my hand. Go on. Tell me.

"Just the leash makes me happy. You don't have to do anything more if you don't want to."

I shook my head. I needed her to understand that this absolutely wasn't about charity.

Letting my touch become more forceful, I swept my hand down her neck, fingering the collar as I did. Mine. The word roared through my mind, shocking me with its force. I knew lead and collar was one of Kristina's favorite fetishes. It had never done much for me as a bottom, so I'd thought I wasn't into it. Tonight, I was learning that a change of perspective could change my opinion.

Kristina had lowered her eyes again, her nostrils

quivering as she breathed. I felt greedy for her attention.

Hooking my first finger through the ring at the front of her collar, I pulled hard. Her gaze snapped to mine. From there, I moved boldly—fingers to her collarbone, pressing enough to remind her of how delicate that spot is. She stood straighter, shrugging her shoulders back, jutting her breasts forward.

I let my hand fall onto her bare left breast, watching carefully for any sign of discomfort.

Kristina's eyes widened, but she didn't move.

Okay?

"Yes." Kristina whispered the word, so I couldn't hear it, but I recognized the shape she made with her lips.

I shifted down to the nipple, trying to let her see the lust on my face. I wanted her to know this wasn't a pity fuck. This was about Max wanting to use the woman he was leading around on a leash, and about me wanting to step into that fantasy and be him. With luck, Kristina wanted the same.

I teased her nipple with the palm of my hand until it turned pebble-hard.

Okay?

"Yes. Please..." She slanted her eyes up at me while her lips took on a sly curl. "Please, Master..."

Clever girl. If I was reading her right, that was a permission slip for more than the sensual overtures I'd been making. I took it as a request for a firmer, kinkier hand.

I turned my teasing touch into a hard pinch. Kristina gasped, but this time she didn't need my questioning signal to tell me how she felt about what I'd done.

"Yes," she moaned, as her body jerked. "Yes. Please, Master."

Also new to my list of fetishes: being called master. That was doing something special to me, making that silicone cock in my pants come to life. I could have sworn I felt it twitching.

I wanted to go all-out now, but I needed a little more information. I snapped my fingers in front of her face to make sure I had her attention, and then trailed my fingers down her stomach, approaching the line of her pubic hair.

Okay?

Kristina widened her legs. "It's your pussy, Master."

I was glad I was supposed to be silent because I would have been speechless either way. The arousal I felt as she opened to me was making me swell all over. My breath caught on the way to my lungs. My fingers trembled and buzzed.

I grazed her pubic hair with the tip of my smallest finger, because any more would have made me lose control entirely. She gasped at the contact, and so did I. Even her hair was soaked with her wetness.

One last piece of information, and I could have my way with her. I lifted my end of the leash, and then slapped it against one of my palms, sharply enough to sting. I did it three times, not holding back, and raised an eyebrow.

"Oh," Kristina said. She sank to her knees and pressed her face against my thigh. "Yes. I want it. I want it all, Master. Please. Whatever you want to do to me, I want it."

She sounded as desperate as I felt. My chest was so tight with need that it was as if I'd never had a voice in the first place. Max was, quite literally, unspeakably sexy. I was so glad to be him.

I'd done my due diligence. That might not have been my usual method for negotiation, but at this point I felt very confident I had Kristina's full consent. I allowed myself a moment to savor the feeling of her at my feet. She had curled her fingers into a fold of my tuxedo pants, and I liked the sight of her clinging to me.

If I hadn't been silent tonight, I might have felt weird about letting the moment stretch, but I was discovering a power to this. Inside the void created by the absence of words, I could hear the pounding of my own heart, could feel the throbbing of my need, could practically smell Kristina getting even wetter for me.

When I was good and ready, I hauled her up with the leash. She was in deep now, her eyes fogged with lust, her movements loose.

Gripping her as close to the collar as I could, I pulled her face to mine and kissed her aggressively, like I owned her. For tonight, as Max, I did.

I made sure she knew it, forcing my tongue deep, controlling her with one hand on the leash and one hand in her hair, pushing her off-balance and forcing her to rely on me to hold her up.

At another time, I might have stopped to wonder at what I was doing, kissing my best friend like that. Tonight, the persona of Max was taking me over. He wasn't the type to wonder.

I kissed Kristina until I felt her body surrender in my arms, and at that moment, I broke away, though I steadied her as she stumblingly regained her footing. We both had to catch our breath a bit after that, and I took the opportunity to scan for some free furniture.

The suspension frames were all in use, and each one had drawn a crowd. There was an intense-looking needle scene taking place on a massage table, and the people on both St. Andrew's Crosses were caught in complicated webs of rope that suggested they'd be there for a while. In a far corner, though, I spotted a spanking bench. Simple, effective, and perfect because I hadn't brought much in the way of equipment.

I marched Kristina toward it, deliberately pulling her one way and then the other, reminding her with every step that she wasn't in control. I knew my friend had been on a spanking bench before, but I didn't let her place herself there. Directing each of her limbs, I arranged her, acting as if it mattered that she put her hands in exactly those particular spots, and that her knees wind up just so. She ended up on all fours over the bench, her torso supported by a padded crossbar, her naked ass raised for my attention. I plucked the leash gently to remind her of the collar, and to show her that I hadn't let her go.

I watched her lungs expand and contract as her body relaxed into position. The sight of her giving herself over to submission made me hot and feral again. I wanted to take my cock out and fuck her right there, but Max was smoother than that and we both knew it. I had to live up to the fantasy we'd wandered into.

I put my hand on the small of her back and pressed firmly, signaling her to stay. Kneeling by Kristina's face, I made the okay gesture one more time, just to check. She nodded blissfully. I could see Max reflected in her eyes, and god was he hot. I adjusted my trousers just to feel the bulge move, just to remind myself that the sexy guy Kristina was melting for was me.

Then I curled my fingers over her left hand and showed her how I wanted her to signal to me. Thumbs up for good. Thumbs down for not good. Just in case I couldn't hear her while she was facedown at a crowded party.

She put both thumbs up and wiggled her ass. "Master, please..."

That was my cue to get started. I grinned, kissed her on the forehead, stood up, and took my sweet time walking around to her ass. I liked listening to the chain clinking as I moved, and more than that, I liked knowing she needed me so badly.

The hosts of the party had thoughtfully outfitted each piece of kink furniture with an end table covered in useful supplies. I took stock as I sauntered. Wipes, lube, gloves, condoms... I'd signed the consent form at the door as a formality, only barely taking notice of the details—penetration was allowed, fireplay wasn't, and so on. I hadn't thought any of that would apply to me.

Now, though, I was glad to see the condoms. I let one hand play over the front of my tuxedo pants. I might be using them before this night was over, and the thought gave me a shiver.

Kristina was trembling on the spanking bench. I rested a hand on her ass and just enjoyed the vibration. I'd been there as a bottom, so excited that the nervous energy came pouring out of me. I knew that when I gave her the pain it would settle her nerves. I promised myself that I wouldn't fuck her until I'd well and truly turned her to jelly. Max struck me as that type of guy.

I started the spanking slow. The implement at the end of the leash was hers not mine, and I wanted to give myself a chance to understand its movement before I started laying in. The first few strokes, the leather slapper only kissed her bare skin. It said hello lightly, causing little more than soft ripples through her generous curves.

She began moaning right away, her back arching, her ass straining up for more. I pulled the leash taut to remind her that she wasn't the one setting the pace. Kristina stilled.

I continued warming up, tapping each of her cheeks steadily but softly, waiting for her dark skin to begin to blush a little. Gradually, a rosier color came over her ass. I felt her with my palm, and she'd gotten even hotter. It was time to try a harder stroke.

I did it once, across the backs of her thighs, letting the leather rest against her skin at the end, connecting us. The blow reverberated up into my elbow, and I watched it pass through her body, too, eventually released from her mouth as a sharp, near-orgasmic moan.

She lifted a thumb, and I petted her ass to thank her for remembering to signal, and then rewarded her with another hard strike.

God, I loved the way she cried out. She sounded so surprised and pleased, as if she'd just won concert tickets on the radio. If I'd played the sound out of context, no one would ever have guessed it was caused by the vicious slap of leather against her bare bottom.

I went up and down her thighs. I covered both cheeks of her ass. I watched red lines and patches of red dots rise on her dark skin, and the pleasure never went out of her voice. Indeed, I could see her arousal trickling down her inner thighs. I wanted to touch her there so badly, but I forced myself to wait a little longer.

Her breaths were long and even. Her face was turned to one side, but I could see the way her cheek was shaped by a broad grin. She held both thumbs up to give me approval. She was having the time of her life.

The feral part of me wanted to push her harder though. Kristina's submission and pleasure were lovely, but the extent to which she was giving herself to me made me crave a little more edge. I wanted to see her struggle to give me what I wanted, to be tempted to pull away but then surrender to me anyway. I wanted that last signal that she was mine for tonight before I gave in and fucked her.

So the next time she rolled her hips and whimpered, showing me her pussy and obviously begging for my fingers or my cock, I let her have the strap there instead.

She grunted from deep in her throat, momentarily frozen. I was entranced by the glimpse I'd caught of a fully aroused cunt, swollen and purple with need. I waited for the thumbs up, and hit her there again. She writhed with the blow, and I could tell that Kristina couldn't decide if it hurt or made her want to come. I wanted it to be both.

Hitting her pussy was an entrancing peep show. With each strike, more tantalizing signs of her arousal revealed themselves. A light spray of her wetness as the leather made contact. A desperate wiggle of her hips that opened her pussy even wider. A twitch that went up her inner thighs and made her entrance wink open and closed.

Kristina moaned constantly now, whether I was hitting her or not. She had squeezed her eyes shut. Her fists clenched and unclenched, though her thumbs remained lifted.

I couldn't take this anymore. She was so beautiful this way, ass all red, cunt wide open, expression inward with pain and need, head resting against the bench's support, collar and lead still fastened. I grabbed for a glove and snapped it onto my hand. Then I brought the slapper end of the leash, wet with her juices, around to her face.

She opened her mouth automatically when it arrived, licking herself off the leather, still moaning. That overwhelmed me, too. I yanked the leather away and replaced it with my gloved fingers.

She sucked them, her red-hot tongue slithering over the tips, then between them, then down to the webbing at the base of them. It made me want to see what she did with my cock right now, but I needed one more confirmation.

With the hand that held the slapper, I caught her by the jaw to get her attention, noticing how pretty her face looked next to the leather instrument I'd used to beat her rosy. Then I pulled my fingers out of her mouth and made the okay gesture one last time.

"God yes," Kristina said. "Fuck me. Use me, Master." She grabbed at the bulge in the front of my tuxedo pants, but was too uncoordinated from the spanking to do much with it. I had a moment of the most intense gratitude that I'd gone all out and purchased that cock for myself.

I kissed her hard, grabbing handfuls of her body as I did, squeezing them to the point of pleasure-pain. It felt incredible to be standing while she was on all fours on this bench, to be clothed while she was naked, to be holding her leash while she was collared.

I returned to her ass, admiring it once more, tracing the marks I'd left on her, feeling the heat of it all. Then I plunged into her pussy with one finger. She was so wet that I quickly realized I didn't need to work up to anything. One finger became two, then three. I knelt on the floor to change my angle so I could work her clit with my thumb at the same time.

She moaned now like I was beating her, and if I'd played that recording out of context, a person would have assumed she was sobbing from pain, not coming so hard that it felt like she might snap the bones in my hand.

I wanted inside her even more deeply. I couldn't stop thinking about my cock. I'd used a strap-on before, but this felt different. I was Max now. The thing in my pants wasn't a toy I was putting on. It was part of me.

I fucked Kristina until my arm got tired, partly because, much as I wanted to pull out the cock, I was scared of how much I might feel when I did. After the second time she came, though, she started begging for it: "Master, give me your cock."

Another thing I'd need to add to my list of fetishes in the future. I cupped it through my pants. Beneath the cock, my clit felt like it had doubled in size. It was throbbing so hard I thought it might burst.

I discarded my glove, grabbed a condom from the end table, opened my pants, took out my cock, and rolled it on. Workman-like as those actions were, they set my body on fire. Each of those practical movements sealed my identity as Max into my head. I was a handsome, sexy, well-put-together, dominant man, about to give his submissive the fucking of her life.

I lubed up and thrust into her, hard and fast, because I knew she was ready.

"Fuck," Kristina said, her voice low and growling now. "Fuck, Master, your cock feels so good."

I didn't let myself make any noise. Any sounds from me would have ruined everything. I closed my throat so tight I almost held my breath, and I grabbed Kristina by the hips, her leash still gripped in my left hand, and fucked her as hard as I could.

Her reddened ass rolled with my every stroke. Her hands scrabbled for purchase against the spanking bench. I wrapped the leash in my fist, shortening it until she had to lift her head and arch her back as I drove into her. Her neck was beautiful; her hair was beautiful; her face was so beautiful. I couldn't believe I was inside this woman, that she was giving herself to me so completely, that I was taking her body with my cock and witnessing how much she loved it.

My sensations were entirely confused. Cock, clit, cunt—whatever I had in my pants, all of it was turned on beyond belief. Every instinct I had told me to drive into Kristina. I did. And when I came, my head throbbed and my eyes closed and my heart opened and I felt myself release into her.

Sweat ran off her naked sides and onto the spanking bench.

My clothes—both what I owned and what I'd rented—were entirely soaked from my exertions. She was half-laughing and half-sobbing, and I was gasping, half from pleasure and half from disorientation.

Carefully, I pulled out of her, disposed of the condom, tucked my cock away. I hugged her, stroked her hair, kissed her again and again. Then we wiped off the bench, cleaned up our mess, and retired to the room with refreshments, still flushed and stunned.

We stayed hours after that, watched other people's scenes, and touched each other shyly from time to time, but finally the party shut down and we had to return to our normal lives. I didn't want to speak until I'd gotten out of Max's clothes, didn't want to break the spell before I absolutely had to. Kristina seemed to understand, and we drove in smiling silence back to my apartment.

Taking off my clothes felt more like putting them on again. As my female body emerged from the binder, as I stripped away Max's cock, I saw the way she looked at me starting to change. The lust fell out of her eyes, and I was just Maddie again, just her best friend, not the person who'd made her squeal with lust and squirt her orgasms all over my expensive rented vest.

I excused myself, washed my hands and face, unpinned my hair, took some deep breaths, and murmured my legal name to myself a few times under my breath. I put on my girliest nightgown, taking a moment to observe the shape of my breasts, to see the softness in my face, to watch my eyes lose Max's wolfish gleam. Only then did I return to the living room, where Kristina sat on my couch with my open laptop, browsing through my streaming video account.

She greeted me with a smile—but not a lover's smile.

"I was thinking we could order a pizza," she said.

"We'll have to order two," I said. "You know we can never agree on the toppings." My voice did exactly what I'd feared it would. Unmistakably feminine, it shattered the last of my sense of myself as Max. It returned me to my usual presentation. It dispelled the feeling that my best friend Kristina was my sexual plaything and lover.

I forced back a sudden sense of sadness at the change. Kristina patted the couch beside her. I sat next to her, and she leaned into me. She smelled of coconut and lime and sex and Max, and somehow Max didn't smell quite like me, though I remembered carrying that smell.

I wrapped an arm around her and stroked her hair. After a moment, she kissed my cheek, the way a friend would. It was hard to believe that hours before I'd devoured her mouth and she'd called me master.

"Everything okay?" Kristina asked. "That didn't make things weird, did it?"

I shrugged. "That... I'm going to be thinking about that for a while. But I love you. We're going to be okay."

She sighed. "Maddie, like this, I'm not attracted to you. Is that bad? Were you—"

"I never thought about you that way before tonight.

Being Max was an experience."

"Let's get that pizza," she said. I watched her walk away, watched the ass I'd so admired at the party as it shifted under her clothes.

Right now, as Maddie, I didn't feel lust for her. I didn't know I'd carried such a different person inside me, didn't know that I would feel so much from presenting as male. I listened to her order, leaning my head back against the arm of the couch. I was me now, back to normal, happy to eat pizza with Kristina and watch movies. But I could feel Max inside me now, too, rattling around at the base of my rib cage. I could feel what it was like to have a big, ready cock, and to want to fuck my best friend silly while I spanked her and held her by a leash.

She came back to the couch and curled up next to me. I spooned with her, my face buried in her hair.

"Maddie?" Kristina murmured after a minute.

"Yeah?"

"Would you ever do that again, though? Put on those clothes, I mean, and be Max."

I swallowed. For a second, even though I wasn't wearing it, I could feel that cock stirring. "Yeah. I would. And if I did I might want to do some of the same things."

"Good," Kristina said. "You're my best friend, Maddie. Max, on the other hand—he's hot as fuck. The sort of guy you can't resist calling, even if you maybe know better."

She glanced at me over her shoulder, vulnerability in her eyes. I smiled, stroking her cheek somewhere between the way I would do it and the way Max would have done it. "He's a good guy, I think," I said. "I think he'd like to get that call." I paused and cleared my throat. "And I think I'm going to straight out buy a tuxedo, not rely on rentals."

WHAT MARRIAGE IS ABOUT
by Dale Cameron Lowry

In hindsight, it probably hadn't been the best idea to bring it up in the heat of the moment, with his pants pushed down to his knees and his cock in Ed's hand. But that was exactly why Darren forgot himself. Ed had been off at a linguistics conference in Amsterdam for a week, and seeing him saunter out of the airport like the hot Euro-chic professor he was—his mustard jeans clinging to his hips and showing off his bulge, his Oxford shirt with the rolled up sleeves hugging tight across his chest, his horn-rimmed glasses framing alert eyes and his upswept hair slightly disheveled from the long flight— had given Darren a raging hard-on.

Darren was so turned on his body thrummed like a vacuum cleaner, a constant purr that made his skin tingle and his hair stand on end. He'd started tugging off his clothes as soon as they'd shut the front door. Never mind their beagle mutt Penny nosing at Ed's feet. She could have him later. Right now, Darren wanted to be stripped bare, to let Ed's lips and hands and cock reclaim him.

They somehow made it to the bed, Darren on his

back and arching up into Ed's touch, perilously close to coming and not caring if he did. A lot of times that made it even better, made his muscles relax, made the pleasure of turning his body over for Ed's use more acute. Ed's breath was hot on his face, and his own breath felt hot too as he moaned, crackling like fire against his sternum, searing his throat. His chest vibrated, his mouth hung open. His vocal chords felt raw already, and he wondered for a moment how loud he was being before reminding himself it didn't matter. They lived in a freestanding house now, and the windows were closed. No need to worry about people upstairs or on the other side of the walls complaining about that loud Deaf couple that knew nothing about volume control.

I missed you, Ed signed with his right hand as he continued to work Darren with his left, using his thumb to slick Darren's precome down the underside of his dick. A cry rattled Darren's ribcage and made his neck buzz. He was undone.

I love you. Darren used the one-handed version of the phrase, signed as a single word. He loved how compact it was, that such an enormous feeling could be condensed into something so small.

Ed's eyes went wide and glazed when he looked down at Darren's cock. He had a tendency to get mesmerized by Darren's body during sex, by the motion of their bodies together. *Hot,* he signed as Darren's slit oozed out another bead of precome.

Darren fucked into Ed's touch, trying to spread his

legs wider to show Ed where else he wanted him—but the pants around his knees kept him shackled, which was even hotter than showing Ed what he wanted, which made Darren hungry for what he *really* wanted, even more than Ed's hands and tongue and dick on him and in him. He needed something to ground him, something to hold him still, to keep him from spinning apart. Needed the thing he'd only dared hint at before. He nudged Ed's chin. *Tie my wrists to the headboard.*

Ed sprang back like someone had stuck him with a livewire. *You're not serious!*

I am.

You don't try to negotiate kinks in the middle of fucking! Especially not ones like that! Ed stabbed wielded his words like sai swords, his hands slicing through the air. His nose wrinkled up as if Darren smelled like a gutted pig, all entrails and decay.

Calm down.

I love you. How can you ask me to do that to you? Ed used the old-fashioned form of *I love you*, the one that required three words and two hands, and looked like the German Sign Language words he'd grown up with. That was the language of Ed's childhood and heart, and when Ed's accent slipped, it usually made Darren swoon, got him feeling like he was being invited into Ed's inner world. But now the words were dangerous. Ed jabbed at his chest when he said *I*, and when he said *you*—well, if being pissed off could make lightning shoot out from a person's fingertips, Darren would have been incinerated.

There were more words. Stupid words. Careless ones. Words that neither of them thought out before letting them fly from their hands. Ed stormed out of the room, slamming the door behind him. The air pressure shifted, unsettling one corner of the top sheet. The wedding picture that hung on the wall jerked askew.

Darren groaned and fell back on the bed, his hard-on no longer so raging. He looked down at it. For one nanosecond, he considered jacking off. It wasn't like Ed was going to come back to finish the job. But the thought of masturbating had the paradoxical effect of making Darren's dick shrink even more, and pretty soon it was back to its usual state, soft and wrinkly like a miniature pug taking a nap on his balls, and fuck it all. He needed to go talk to Ed.

Darren pulled his pants up and tugged his little pug-dick away, holding one hand over it as he worked the zipper. He hadn't even put on underwear before picking up Ed from the airport, so certain he'd been that they'd end up in the bedroom as soon as they got home.

***

There was a reason Darren had never mentioned this particular desire, just let it simmer under his skin until everything became too hot and it roiled, blowing the lid off and spilling out in a sudden splash, scalding what it touched: spouses don't ask their spouses to relive their worst childhood memories.

Ed woke up in a sweat sometimes from the

nightmares. *Silly*, he would say. *I should be over that by now*. It didn't keep them from coming. He'd dream he was back in his little school for the hearing impaired in what had then been East Germany, being punished for signing by having to sit on his hands through the rest of class, his wrists aching, his fingers going cold and then numb. He needed to pee, or he was having a heart attack, but every time he moved his hands to speak up he'd get whacked with the ruler before the first word got out.

Sometimes it was his mother, who'd gone through a phase of tying his wrists behind his back if he signed by accident, worried that leniency would make him unfit for the Hearing world.

Being forbidden from signing hadn't made it any easier to read people's lips when they spoke, made it even harder to form the same gibberish with his mouth. With his hands restrained, he couldn't concentrate on the movements his cheeks and lips were supposed to make, forgot to imagine a lead weight pulling down on his chin when he said *a* or holding a coin between the tip of his tongue and the roof of his mouth when he said *i* or *ü*. In his dreams, his mother cared about that as much as she had in real life, which was not at all. The fact that his lips were moving was what mattered. His teachers would pause and correct him with their own garbled lip motions, sometimes touching his face with clammy palms and cold fingers to force it into the right shape, and all the while he had to sit there and take it—couldn't push them away, couldn't tell them what he thought of their nonsense mouth language, couldn't tell them to fuck off in words that anyone could see plain as day.

Darren was lucky. He was a Deaf kid of Deaf parents, born after academics recognized American Sign Language as a real language and bilingual education had become the standard in U.S. schools for the Deaf. Learning English could be a pain in the ass sometimes, but so could math. No one ever restrained Darren's hands or told him that mouth-language was the only right way to speak.

For Darren, hand restraints weren't a symbol of oppression. They were a natural outgrowth of his desires. He liked the feeling of being controlled and contained, liked sex best when Ed's weight was on him, squeezing the air from his lungs, Ed's thighs and chest trapping him against the mattress. He liked when his movements were limited. It stripped away the pressure of always having to *go* and *do*, gave him no choice but to simply *be*. In those moments he was his purest self, and he was Ed's completely.

Darren had talked Ed into tying his ankles to the footboard a few months before, his legs spread and his stomach flat on the mattress, Ed fucking him from behind. But Ed hadn't been so into it, didn't like that he could only see half of Darren's face and that the position made signing awkward and hard to see.

We hardly sign anyway when we're fucking, Darren had countered.

But we sign a little. I kept worrying you were

uncomfortable.

How could you think I was uncomfortable? It was so good I was biting the pillow.

Biting isn't always a sign of pleasure.

It is for me.

But Darren let it go. Back-to-front fucking wasn't a necessary part of his kink. It was the restraint that did him in. So the next time he brought it up, he asked Ed to tie his ankles to the headboard instead.

You mean, fold you in half?

Darren smirked. *You usually end up folding me in half anyway.*

I guess I do. I'm lucky to have a dancer as a husband. So flexible.

Ed gave the scarves some slack, but not too much. Darren's ankles burned when he tried to move, to influence the rhythm or the ankle—so he stopped trying. And that's when it got good, when he stopped trying to thrust himself on Ed's dick—stopped seeking out more friction, more movement, a stronger slide against his prostate. He lay there and took whatever Ed was ready to give him, took it until Ed was right on the edge, murmuring *I love you* with one hand and wrapping the other around Darren's cock to strip it in time with his ass. Ed's features stiffened when he came, his eyes wide with something like shock as he shot into Darren's body, and when Ed collapsed onto Darren's chest he came too, splattering their skin.

Darren felt it all the next day at rehearsal, his thighs

screaming with every movement.

It felt wonderful.

The next time Darren asked for bondage, Ed responded eagerly—to a point. He'd been researching it in the meantime, reading on the internet about different kinds of knots and cloth and rope. *I had no idea there were so many ways to tie a person up*, he'd said. *Thought bondage was all about handcuffs, which of course I could never get into.*

The words landed sour in Darren's stomach like too-strong coffee, but he didn't let them spoil his mood. *Because of your first Deaf school?*

And my mom in her crazy phase. I can see why Hearing people might be into it, but they don't sign.

Hearing people do gags. Isn't that the same thing?

No. They don't have teachers who tape their mouths shut because speaking is low-class.

Darren dropped it. He was still getting tied up, so why let himself feel like he was losing out? And if he couldn't keep his unbound hands from signing *harder, faster, slower, softer,* and if Ed teased him that he was a bossy little minx but complied anyway—well, he'd just hold onto something—Ed's shoulders or his ass or the small of his back—anything to keep himself from trying to choreograph the dance.

Of course, holding onto Ed's body led to directing it. Darren pushed and pulled, tugged and twisted, only realizing as one or the other of them came that he'd defeated his own purposes.

Still, it wasn't like ankle-tying was the only kink they engaged in. They liked biting and leaving purple bruises where no one but them would ever see. When they'd lived in the apartment, Ed had developed a penchant for gagging Darren, pretending at first it was for the pure utility of keeping down complaints from the neighbors, but obviously getting off on the way it made Darren drool. And Darren had warmed Ed up to the idea of spanking him with the gag on, first with gentle slaps and then, as he became more comfortable with it, sharp, stinging cracks that made him grind his teeth into the cloth until, over the course of several sessions, it finally frayed.

It should have been enough. It was, by any objective standard, plenty.

And still Darren wanted.

***

Darren found Ed in the kitchen, making coffee. Stream rose from the pot. The coffee maker's little blue light blinked on-off, on-off to indicate the brew was done. Ed didn't look at it or at Darren. His face was down, his eyebrows furrowed. He opened the silverware drawer, snatched a spoon, then slammed the drawer shut. Next Ed attacked the cupboard, jerking the door open and yanking out a mug. He moved on to assault the refrigerator and the poor hapless sugar bowl. Crystals scattered on the counter. Ed scowled but didn't brush them up. Penny kept close to Ed's heels, looking up with a mix of wariness and optimism in her big brown eyes. Clearly she could see Ed was in a tizzy, but hope sprang eternal in that dog's soul, and if there was any chance he'd drop a scrap of food in his fit of pique, she'd be there to catch it.

Darren was not as optimistic as their dog. He gave Ed a wide berth. Touching him would only startle him, and flicking the kitchen lights would be a demand: Pay attention to me. Darren didn't want to make another demand. Not yet. Marriage was a constant balancing act of knowing when to ask for something right away and when to wait. Darren should have waited earlier, and he could wait now.

It wasn't until Ed sat down at the kitchen table with his coffee and a couple of those weird health-food cookies he liked that he finally caught sight of Darren. He nodded, but didn't smile. *I made enough coffee for both of us, if you want some.*

A truce.

Darren had to slow himself down before he went over there, calm his own nerves so he didn't end up blurting out excuses about not meaning to upset Ed or letting his hands move faster than his brain. He took his time getting out his own mug, pouring in the coffee, and stirring in the half-and-half by dribs and drabs. He shuffled through the contents of the pantry before finally pulling out a bag of potato chips.

Ed raised his brows. *Potato chips and coffee? Interesting.* Still, he smiled—if only for a moment.

Another peace offering.

I have sophisticated tastes.

They didn't say anything more. Penny rubbed against Ed's calves and nuzzled his thigh. Darren looked out the window and watched a woodpecker hop up the side of the ash tree as jerkily as a hiccup. He pointed to it. Ed followed his finger and this time his smile was bigger, spreading to the corners of his eyes. He kept smiling even after it flew away.

Ed petted Penny's head. His cookie plate had only crumbs now. His mug was empty. So was Darren's.

I'm sorry, Ed said. *I've had a long week, and a long flight. I overreacted.*

I'm sorry too. I got too horny. I wasn't thinking.

You mean, you said something you didn't mean? Or you weren't thinking about whether it was the right time to say it?

I... meant it.

OK. Ed's look was inscrutable. Darren wondered if it was the same look he gave students when they had the wrong answer.

Is it really OK?

I don't know. Ed's eyes gentled. *On the bright side, I make you too horny to think.*

Darren felt his face warm. Eleven years and Ed could still make him blush like a schoolboy. *It's not that hard to make me forget to think. I never was as smart as you, professor.*

If you want to do teacher-student roleplay, handcuffs

are definitely not an option. Ed wasn't flirting anymore, but he wasn't scowling either. A good omen.

Aren't they always off-limits though? With your history?

Ed scooted his chair back. It gave him more signing room. Another good omen. He wasn't about to end the conversation. *I don't know. It's my issue. Not yours. Can you explain it to me, though? Why you'd want your hands bound?*

It's the same as with tying my feet. I like when you're in control. And I like the idea of not being able to tell you what I want. I can get bossy sometimes. I want you to boss me.

You put a lot of trust in me.

You've earned it.

Ed's eyes softened. He stood and pulled Darren to his feet, kissing him gently—lips only, no tongue. It made Darren's cock spring up against Ed's hip. Ed pulled back. *Still horny? Arguing didn't kill it for you?*

I told you I missed you.

Enough for a good old-fashioned vanilla fuck?

Definitely.

They went back to the bedroom. Darren wasn't sure the vigor with which Ed tongued his ass could be strictly categorized as *vanilla*, but it was nothing out of the ordinary for them. It felt different, though. With his desire out in the open, Darren was almost as splayed and vulnerable as he would have been if he were tied spread-eagle on the bed. He came so hard his skull shook.

Afterward they lay on their backs, their legs tangled as they caught their breath. Darren thought a breeze would feel nice, but he liked Ed's skin too much to go open the window.

Ed rolled onto one elbow but kept his leg curled around Darren's thigh. *Give me time?*

You have me forever already.

Ed laughed. *I'll try not to take that long.*

***

They sat facing each other on the couch, one of them at each end, their legs overlapping in the middle with Penny on top. Ed had his laptop out. Darren was watching clips of the *Spring Awakening* Broadway revival on his phone and rubbing Penny behind the ears.

Ed closed his laptop and tapped Darren's ankle. *I'm ready.*

For what? Were they supposed to go somewhere? Did they have an appointment that Darren had forgotten?

Ed flushed. *To try hand restraints.*

Darren dropped his phone. Penny startled and pricked her ears.

They hadn't talked about this since that ill-fated post-Amsterdam argument, though it continued to hang between them. Ed would get this knowing smile when they fucked and Darren grabbed the rails to keep himself from talking, and a week earlier Ed had interlaced the fingers of his right hand through Darren's left while they fucked. It wasn't something that would have inhibited

Darren from signing, but he got the sense that Ed was playing his own boundaries, testing to see if even this most benign form of restraint would be too difficult to fuck through.

It hadn't been—not for Darren and apparently not for Ed, whose face went from hesitant to relieved as he continued fucking into Darren, then from relieved to enthusiastic as Darren came, then finally ecstatic as his own orgasm washed over him. Afterward, his expression was that of someone proud of their own prowess.

Darren had chosen not to remark on it at the time. He didn't trust himself to listen objectively to whatever Ed had to say about the experience, or to keep from teasing, *Oh you liked that, well you'll like handcuffing me even more*. He didn't want to accidentally turn his enthusiasm into pressure or cajoling. Discussion wasn't the best way to get Ed to come around on things. He needed to store them in an undisturbed corner of his mind where he could chew on them without interference from others.

Are you sure? Darren said.

I'm sure I want to try. I can't promise it will work. But I like getting you hot. And this gets you hot, doesn't it?

Darren wasn't going to deny it. His cock was stirring as they spoke, transforming from sleeping pug puppy to stiff sausage.

They started that night, with a scarf around Darren's left wrist. His right hand was his dominant one, so the restraint couldn't prevent him from signing any more than holding a cup of coffee would—less so, because he could still make shapes with it even if he couldn't move it around. But that's what made Ed willing to tie the knot, and it didn't keep Ed from asking about a million times if Darren was OK.

We don't have to do this, Darren signed after his dozen *yes*ses didn't get through. (Maybe it was only three, but since his fantasy involved not being able to talk at all, it felt like more.)

Ed smirked. *Yes we do.*

Oh?

I'm determined to learn what this is about. And holding your left hand down last week turned out OK.

I'd been wondering if that was a test.

Yes. And it didn't freak me out the way I'd worried it would. You looked so turned on getting restrained. It was hard for me to associate what I was doing to you with my own baggage. I realized—he started to laugh—*you're not me.* Ed took Darren's right hand in his own and guided it to the headboard, coaxing Darren's fingers around the center rail. *There. You can pretend I've tied both hands if you want. A compromise.*

Darren's previous irritation softened, and when Ed trailed his own hands down his chest to tweak his right nipple, it evaporated. Irritation? What irritation? Darren arched off the bed, unaware of any emotion that wasn't pleasure.

Ed let go, the tease. *So part of what you like about this idea, about not being able to sign, is that I make all the decisions? I decide what to do to you?*

Darren nodded.

So I could do this as much as I want? Ed pinched the nipple again, causing Darren to jerk into the mattress as he nodded.

And I can make you come by sucking you off, or fingering you, or licking your ass, or riding your cock, or fucking you until the bed breaks? Whatever I want?

Darren nodded through every question, his dick throbbing. He gripped the headboard rail tighter to keep from telling Ed which ones he wanted, clenched his bound left hand into a fist so he wouldn't start fingerspelling the answer in English: All of them, preferably at once.

God, Ed made him greedy.

Ed drew his hands closer to his body the way he would in public when he didn't want anyone but Darren to see whatever words he was about to say. *Or maybe I shouldn't worry about you coming at all? Do you want me to use you to get off?*

Darren's mouth dropped open. Vibrations ripped through his throat.

The sparkle in Ed's eyes made it clear he saw the *yes* in Darren's. He swooped down and kissed the fingers of Darren's bound hand, mouthing at the tip of each one before moving to his wrist to brush his lips on either side of the scarf they were using as a restraint. Darren shivered when Ed jutted out his tongue to drag it along the sensitive skin of his inner forearm; it was so light it felt almost like a tickle and evoked that same strange alien sense of just-right and too-much that tickling did, that pleasure so intense it needed to be escaped. But he didn't flinch. He kept his right hand on the rail as securely as if Ed had handcuffed him there, and when Ed moved to the soft spot on the inside of his left elbow and then down to his supremely ticklish armpit, he giggled and snorted but didn't squirm away—and soon his giggling and snorting became something else, something charged and erotic as he gave up on even the idea of resistance.

Darren's nipples pebbled and his cock throbbed and grew, and he felt Ed's growing, too, hard and hot against his thigh.

Ed continued kissing down Darren's body, watching Darren's face as he trailed his tongue into Darren's navel and raked his fingers over Darren's chest. He caught the coarse hairs that grew around Darren's nipples and tugged hard. *Yes,* Darren wanted to sign as each needle-sharp spark of pain moved through his skin, and *More,* but he could only nod his head into the pillow and let his ever-expanding cock speak for him.

Ed teased it with his chin and neck before taking it in his mouth with a swift, mind-shattering suck, his mouth wet and hot and tight as a vacuum cleaner. *Stop or I'll come,* Darren thought, but he didn't sign it.

Maybe it wouldn't be so bad if he came, anyway. Coming was good. Coming was awesome. And maybe this was his only chance.

He instinctively moved his hips toward Ed's face. Ed pinned them down.

Darren groaned in frustration. Arousal. The feelings warred in him, and he wasn't sure which was stronger.

Ed sunk his mouth further onto Darren's dick.

Arousal. Arousal was definitely winning.

Ed's mouth grew wetter than wet. Saliva and precome leaked onto the exposed section of Darren's shaft. The square edges of the rail pressed into his palm as he squeezed, resisting the urge to lower his hand into Ed's hair and shove him throat-first onto his dick. The action had a tendency to make Ed feel trapped instead of wanted and, anyway, Darren had no hands for all intents and purposes right now. He had to take whatever Ed would give him.

Ed continued to watch Darren's face as he ran his tongue up and down the underside of Darren's shaft, working closer and closer toward his balls until his glans pressed up against Ed's throat. It was in as far as it would go, and it felt heavenly. Darren's patience had earned this reward.

Ed swallowed and then, his eyes glimmering with mischief, opened his throat and took a little more.

Darren's own eyes bulged. He felt dizzy down to his balls. So much heat, so much tightness around his dick, and then Ed did this little undulating motion with his throat and grabbed Darren's hips to pull him in deeper, and that was it—Darren's semen churned and blasted free. He watched as Ed continued to suck him, swallowing some and letting the rest drip down Darren's hard length onto his pubes and balls. It looked incredibly dirty and incredibly hot, made Darren feel almost as if another orgasm was about to whirl through him. A shuddering aftershock ran up his spine.

Ed pulled off. A trickle of saliva and come dripped from the corner of his mouth. His smile was self-satisfied. *You liked that?*

Darren nodded.

And how about this? Ed crawled over Darren and kissed him, tugging his lips open and licking the residual semen into Darren's mouth. His hand flew over his cock—Darren couldn't see it directly, but he could see Ed's shoulder quivering from the effort, feel his body and the bed shaking in time with Ed's movements. His breath grew more erratic, spasms of tense energy, his kissing veering wildly between fast tonguing thrusts to no movement at all, until with a final strong puff of air into Darren's mouth he came onto Darren's stomach in messy, hot pulses.

***

Over the next few weeks, they fucked several more times with only Darren's left hand bound. *I have to make sure I'm OK with all different positions*, Ed said. Darren suspected that maybe Ed wasn't being merely prudent, but also a tease. Both possibilities endeared Ed to him even more.

The first time Ed tied Darren by his right wrist—his

left hand was free, making it still possible to sign but less instinctive—Ed decided to bottom from the top, fingering himself open as Darren watched helplessly on. He swayed in slow, sexy circles, lubing himself up with one finger, then two, and kept licking his lips like he was eating something succulent. It took everything Darren had not to tug against the restraint or let go of the rail, to sink his own fingers into the inviting heat of Ed's body.

Ed watched Darren's face as he sank himself partway onto Darren's leaking dick. Ed wasn't a natural-born bottom, but he liked it on occasion, especially when he could control the depth and pace, focusing the angle so Darren's dick brushed across his prostate instead of directly at it, letting Darren enter only in unhurried increments, holding him back from submerging himself balls-deep before Ed was ready for it.

That's it, Ed signed, his eyes going wide, and again, *that's it*, and then a bunch of exquisitely dirty things about the size and shape of Darren's dick and the million things he wanted to do to Darren while Darren just lay there and took it, and even with Ed's ankles hooked around his thighs to keep him from thrusting, with just his crown swallowed up by Ed's tight ass, Darren knew he wouldn't last long. Then Ed started to sink down—a millimeter, a centimeter, an inch—a slow perilous slide that made them both pant and twitch.

Ed worked his prostate against Darren's swollen cock, one hand planted on Darren's chest, the other signing words that turned into half-words and nonsense exclamations as Ed grew more excited. He began to shimmy and then to thrust, plunging up-down up-down, feverish and slick. He wrapped his mumbling hand around his dick and stroked it without rhythm or purpose. Its purple head glistened.

Darren couldn't help but come, and still his arousal grew. Ed's ass became tighter, slicker, convulsing around Darren's spent rod. Ed pumped faster, his movements eased by Darren's semen.

He squeezed his cock and climaxed.

**

We need a safe signal, Ed said three weeks later as they finished washing the dishes. *If you want both your hands tied.*

The comment was apropos of nothing, but Darren wasn't caught off guard. He'd been thinking about the same thing ever since they'd progressed from left- to right-hand binding. *I could fingerspell.*

Ed shook his head. *I might not see it. We need something to get my attention no matter what.*

What about Penny's dog whistle?

Ed laughed. *I'm Deaf, dummy.*

Darren rolled his eyes. *Not for you. For Penny. I blow on the whistle and she comes running to the bed. That would get your attention.*

I don't want to have sex whilst a dog's in the bed.

Perfect safe signal, then. It would stop you right in your tracks.

Why don't you just call her?

My speech therapists always said my pronunciation went to shit when I got excited. Penny might not understand me.

The plan was to have Darren's right hand bound and the left hand free, but with a scarf around it to give him the illusion of being tethered. Ed set the whistle between Darren's teeth and started working on the knots. His fingers were warm and light. Darren gasped and sighed through the whistle's tight aperture.

Penny barreled into the room, leaped front-paws first onto Darren's chest and knocked the wind right out of him. She licked his chin, clearly pleased with herself, then cocked her head the way she always did when she expected a treat.

Dog whistles were out.

Darren picked up Penny, carried her out of the room, and headed for the coat closet to fish out one of the red safety lights they hooked to their jackets for walking Penny after dark. Ed was half-dressed by the time Darren made it back to the bedroom. *What about this? It's bright whichever way you point it, and if I set it to strobe it will definitely get your attention.*

Ed shucked off his pants while Darren was still talking. Darren dimmed the lights halfway.

It worked.

***

They waited for their next shared afternoon off to try it

with both of Darren's wrists bound. Concentration worried Ed's brows as he secured the scarf it to the headboard. He looked at Darren. *You OK?*

Darren lay naked on his back, the blankets folded around his feet, his arms raised above his head, strobe light secure in the palm of his left hand. He was better than OK, bordering on elated. He nodded, then raised his eyebrows and let one last word slip from his right hand. *OK?* He pointed to Ed with his chin.

Yes. Ed smiled. *You're gorgeous like this.*

Usually Darren would try to deflect the compliment. He would say that he wasn't, or that Ed was hotter. But he had no choice now but to simply accept it.

Darren could see Ed registering his discomfort, weighing whether he should ease up on the sweet talk or test Darren's limits. The strobe was for anything, they'd agreed—not just pain and safety, but even if the good became too much.

Not only are you gorgeous, but since I've started tying your wrist to the headboard, I've really developed an attraction to your armpits. They're so sexy ... and vulnerable. With a look of smug satisfaction, Ed dove into Darren's underarm and licked, pushing through Darren's conniptions of laughter until he was panting with need. Darren's dick grew solid and heavy, bouncing against his stomach as he squirmed, but Ed ignored it. He grabbed the lube and sank down between Darren's legs, pushing his thighs up and back to expose Darren's tender hole.

The lube was cold. Darren reflexively clenched. His asshole had ticklishness in common with his armpits, and Darren breathed out a panicked giggle as Ed began to drag his finger over it, first up then down, left then right, then small circles that traced the rim. Darren felt himself relax, the tight wrinkled edges of his entrance become smoother. Ed pressed a fingertip against it; it clenched, then unwound a little more. It was a continual process, an ebb and flow—one moment tight and the next loose and open, and Ed's fingers worked Darren through it, probed him wider, made Darren struggle against the restraints as he fought the urge to beg for more.

Ed brushed his fingers over Darren's prostate and curled the other hand around Darren's cock, and—oh— Darren though he might spend himself before Ed even fucked him properly. His dick gushed precome as Ed increased the pressure; Ed licked his lips and pulled his fingers out.

And then it was Ed's cockhead pushing inside him, thick and slippery and unforgiving. Darren gasped and began to wrap his legs around Ed's waist, ready to pull him in, but Ed was too fast. He caught his hands under Darren's thighs and splayed them out, pressing them toward the mattress to hold Darren still.

Ed was a tease. With Darren immobilized, he sunk his cock in slow as molasses. Ed was in complete control, fucking Darren just the way he wanted.

Darren's dick throbbed harder.

Ed's breath was hot against his skin, Ed's weight heavy on his hips and shoulders, Ed's lips devouring him, Ed's cock stretching him to his limit. Darren ignored the twitching of his own fingers, the instinct to demand *more*. He refused to look beyond the moment, accepting each of Ed's motions as the gift it was. He took in Ed's musky scent and his hard, gorgeous cock and his soft, probing tongue. He tasted Ed's sweat and felt his arousal grow with each panting thrust.

You're mine, aren't you? Ed signed before taking Darren's throbbing dick into his hand.

Darren answered with his body, with the cries that rattled his chest, the aroused clenching of his fists and ass, the precome flowing from his slit.

Show me.

The orgasm slammed into Darren, sending shudders of pleasure through his ass and slick spurts of semen over Ed's hand.

You're mine, Ed signed again as he started to come.

***

You good? Darren signed when Ed unbound him. His wrists were more sore than usual. He must have tugged against the restraints more than he realized.

I'm flying high. How about you? Did I get too possessive?

No. The perfect amount.

Ed kissed his hands. *Thanks for being patient while I worked through my baggage.*

That's what marriage is about, isn't it?

That and fucking. Mostly fucking.

Darren pulled Ed and kissed him until their laughter got in the way.

***

Author's notes: It's always a challenge to decide how to represent another language in an English-language story. Here I adopted the common (but not universal) practice of representing signed speech in italics and without quotation marks. Rather than providing a literal gloss of American Sign Language (ASL) phrases, I represented them in ordinary English, doing my best to avoid idiomatic phrases unless they have a close ASL equivalent. I strove to retain the sense and tone of the discussion I was imagining, but did not attempt to represent the grammar or exact vocabulary of ASL.

ASL and German Sign Language (Deutsche Gebärdensprache, or DGS) are separate languages but share some word similarities because both are historically related to French Sign Language (Langue des Signes Française, LSF), similar to how Spanish and Romanian are both related to Latin. ASL is not related to spoken English or the sign languages used in the United Kingdom, Australia, or New Zealand.

When writing in English, it's common among American Sign Language users to capitalize "Deaf" to refer to a culture or cultural identity, and to write "deaf" when referring specifically to a partial or complete lack of hearing. Similarly, "Hearing" is often capitalized to refer to people or cultural practices, but not capitalized in medical terminology such as "hearing loss" or "hearing impaired." I have reflected these conventions in this story.

STANDING TALL
by Sienna Saint-Cyr

Master put his fingers in my mouth and held it open. Tears welled up in my eyes as the sting of reprimand caught me. He stared at me with his intense eyes. All his disapproval evident as his expression stayed hard and his dominant energy slammed into me.

I looked at the ceiling and focused on the speckled pattern. Then I stared directly at the light in the hall, hoping it would distract me with its brightness. I even tuned in to the sound of the washing machine spinning, but it was useless. Master's breath kept pulling my focus back to his face.

And his scent... I couldn't ignore his sweet and spicy skin. Master always smelled of chocolate and red chilies.

My tears spilled over. I couldn't hold it in anymore. Nor could I tell him I was sorry, because his fingers prevented me from speaking. I'd never seen Master this upset, and it made my heart ache.

I gagged a little as spit built up around his fingers and he lifted them just enough for me to swallow. Then he pushed me back into the wall and pressed his body into me. His lips touched my ear, but he didn't say anything at first. He stood taller instead and used his steady stance to intimidate me.

I wanted to sink to the floor.

"Do I *tolerate* you belittling yourself, girl?"

I shook my head.

"That's right." He removed his fingers and wiped them on my shirt. "I've tried punishing you for this behavior and it doesn't work, does it, girl?"

"No, Master."

Shame filled me. He's such a wonderful Master and I was letting him down. *What was wrong with me?*

"Tonight, you will attend the party with me. You will go as I instruct you to."

"Yes, Master."

My nerves rose instantly. What would he order me to do? I hoped nothing too embarrassing, but he was angry with me, and I knew the kind of punishment heading my way likely included a heavy dose of humiliation.

Master kissed my right breast—or where it used to be anyway—and whispered into my ear again. "Take a long, hot bath. I'll be back at eight to pick you up. I want you in a short dress, low cut in the front and back, form fitting, and no underwear." He stopped talking and looked deep into my eyes. "*No bra.*"

That was it. Panic set in and I began to hyperventilate. Then came deep sobs. My chest moved raggedly as I sucked in my breath.

"Please, Master, no. Don't make me go out without

my bra."

I lowered my gaze, unable to maintain eye contact.

I wanted so badly to be confident even with my missing breast, but it was so hard. I felt like less of a woman. Which I knew was silly. I'd already overcome my body issues and found confidence with my larger, curvier figure. Then through therapy and Master's slow exposure techniques I'd worked through my issues around being seen naked, even with my trauma from being prostituted as a child. But my curves—and breasts specifically—had helped me overcome some of my trauma by making me feel feminine. Sexy. Beautiful...

Now, I didn't know what I felt.

Like less. Only half a woman. That's all I knew.

"You *will* go out as I instruct you to," Master said in a firmer tone. "Unless you can tell me right now that you're a beautiful, feminine Goddess."

"I'm a beaut..." I began, but my words faded. I couldn't lie to Master. I couldn't say something I didn't believe. This was what had gotten me in trouble. I'd said something unkind about myself. Finally, I surrendered. "I'll try, Master."

"Good, girl. Now take your bath. I'll see you later this evening."

Master kissed my lips this time, slow and hard. I felt him all the way to my cunt. I stayed lost in the moment, even as he pulled away and I heard the front door close behind him. My mouth hung slightly open as I calmed my stirrings and re-centered.

The moment I was able to walk again, I headed to the bath and turned on the water. Once it reached maximum heat, I pulled off my yoga pants and top. I looked at my naked body in the mirror.

I still loved myself. I knew I did. Yet I couldn't understand why I felt so terrible about it. I was alive. That should be all that mattered. And it *did* matter, but all that confidence I'd worked so hard to build, was gone.

If only Master waited just a bit longer. Then I'd be healed enough to look into a breast implant. Why did he have to push this now?

I turned away as the weight of shame overcame me.

I added some lavender oil to the bath, climbed into the tub, and closed my eyes upon submersion. I tried to picture myself prior to the surgery, but a specific memory from my childhood kept flooding back instead. I suppressed it quickly. It'd taken years to gain my confidence and that was *before* losing my breast. I didn't need a memory undoing all my hard work. As past and present blurred in my mind, I had to take a deep breath.

I felt wetness under my eyes, but not from the bathwater.

Finding peace with myself again wouldn't be easy.

Time passed quickly as I soaked. I focused all my energy into relaxing. I knew I'd need to be as calm as possible for what was to come. When my water cooled, I got out, dried off, and ventured into my closet.

I found the perfect dress and likely the one Master

had in mind when he instructed me with what to wear. I wondered why he hadn't just told me the specific dress rather than make me figure it out, but I let that go as I slipped it on and headed back to the bathroom to dry my hair.

I spent a long time on my hair and makeup. I hoped that if I decorated myself, fewer people would notice my missing breast. My special bra helped, because it had a fake breast inside it. Aside from the few close friends I'd shared with, no one knew about my surgery or cancer. They were used to my short hair and didn't suspect a thing when I'd shaved it.

Now that it was long enough to be a stylish pixie cut, I'd used deep blueberry blue dye on it. Not even the cute cut or the lovely color made me feel better, though. Added to my concern was the fact that I'd not attended any parties with Master since I'd gotten sick. What if people thought me a snob?

So much to stress about... My only hope was that Master would be merciful as he did what he was planning to do. Facing everyone knowing I'd kept so much from them wasn't going to be easy either. My breast was only half the problem.

I traced my eyelids with the deepest black liner and put on several layers of mascara. Smoky eyes would distract people nicely too. Or so I hoped.

By the time my doorbell rang, I'd completed my look and was ready physically. I didn't know if I'd ever be ready emotionally. It took several deep breaths for me to get to the door. My heart pounded so hard it felt like it was going to leap from my chest. I fought the salty liquid threatening to escape again, as I didn't want to smear my fresh makeup.

I opened the door and the moment I saw Master, I lowered all the way to the ground. I felt his dominance over me and it made me instantly wet for him. Humbled in his presence.

"Good, girl," he said. "Now stand up."

I obeyed, and greeted him with a gentle kiss.

"You look gorgeous." He smiled. Then pushed me further inside the entryway and into the wall once again. He shut the door behind him.

"Thank you, Master."

He pulled something from his back pocket. I saw it right away. It was a ball gag. Then he pulled out an eye mask. He slipped the mask on first.

So much for my smoky eyes.

"Open your mouth."

I obeyed again, but with hesitance. Since finding my voice, I hated gags. Hated not being able to speak... Still, I trusted Master. I didn't fight him as he slipped the gag into place. He pulled me forward until he could reach behind me and fasten it.

"Tonight, you won't be able to see, speak, or even taste anything but the gag in your mouth. You will only be able to smell, hear, and *feel*. You will be silenced until you can speak kindly about yourself. You will be blinded until you can see yourself clearly." He paused and breathed out loudly before continuing. "*This* will change you."

I began crying again. I wanted to run, to scream my safe word now. But I couldn't. I couldn't do that to myself or to Master. I needed to try.

Master slipped a bracelet on me. He shook my hand several times and tiny bells sang a high-pitched song.

"You will shake your wrist twice if you need to speak and ask me to adjust something. You will shake your wrist four times if you hit your stop point. Four shakes equals red. Shake your wrist now and show me what 'I need to talk' is."

I shook it twice.

"Good, girl. Now show me stop."

I shook it four times.

"Good, girl." He kissed my forehead. "Take hold of my arm, girl."

I did as he instructed.

Master led me out of the door and to the car. I heard him open the door and then he helped me inside and buckled me. Then I heard his door open and shut.

He'd done this many times before and I was thankful I lived in a private area of town. Otherwise, the neighbors might think I was being abducted. The notion made me giggle, but only on the inside.

Master drove for a while, chatting to me about his day the entire time. He'd gotten loads of work done. Made several phone calls to new potential girls. He even shared about how he dropped a girl into subspace and had her masturbate over speakerphone. Normally that'd have me wet and squirming, but since the surgery, anything that involved others or public display hadn't done it for me. It only made me feel insecure. Something I'd shared with Master, but he wasn't the sort to give in to insecurity. A fact I appreciated and hated at the same time.

At least my tears had stopped.

I began zoning out the longer we drove, which made me focus on the drool escaping the corners of my mouth. It was humiliating, and I hadn't even gone inside yet.

When we arrived, Master helped me out of the car and escorted me to the door. From the sound of it, this party was taking place at the club. I could only tell by the whacks and moans bouncing off the walls. It was a familiar echo.

The smell of bergamot also caught my attention. The hosts used the essential oil for one of their scenes. It tended to linger. Knowing where I was felt both like a comfort and horror show. People I'd avoided would be here.

Master walked me around and every time he began talking to someone, I curled inward and leaned into him to hide my breast. Master moved to my left side without a word.

I knew it was so I couldn't hide my missing boob.

I whimpered and forced myself to suppress more tears.

"It's okay, girl," he whispered into my ear. "You.

Are. Beautiful." He kissed my forehead, then greeted more people.

I held onto him tightly, which he seemed okay with as long as I didn't hide myself.

So much of my focus was on not hiding that I couldn't comprehend who we were greeting. I'd been going to the club for years and knew each and every patron, yet I recognized no voices. All I heard was my own inner voice, telling me I was hideous. Less. Incomplete.

After a few more greetings he walked me to the back room. I knew what room it was and I knew why he was taking me there. It was the dungeon. Where the hosts kept the cross.

The blood drained from my face as the realization set in, *he was going to put me on display*.

I wanted to fight him. To shake my wrist four times now. But I fought it.

I thought of all the times Master had made me feel better even before the cancer. The times I'd wanted to die and he'd pulled me from suicidal thoughts. I thought of his kisses, his warm touch, the dominant embrace that made me feel safe and loved, and I fought my safe word. I *wanted* to be strong, because Master had put so much time into me. He truly cared, and I knew it with all my heart.

I wanted to try even if it was more for him now than myself.

But I still trembled.

All the way to the cross.

"You will be a good girl now and remind me of your safe word."

I shook my wrist four times.

"Good, girl."

Master reached for the bottom of my dress and pulled it up. And that's when I heard it... The chatter—the sounds of others entering the dungeon—and my panic got worse.

I didn't lift my arms for him. I squeezed them to my chest instead.

He pinched my thigh hard and flipped me around. Then pushed me forward until I made contact with what I assumed was their massage table. The coolness of the padded surface calmed me slightly, as did hearing Master's bag unzip. The sound dropped me into subspace.

Master pushed my dress up again until my bare ass was facing him and anyone else standing behind us. I let myself drop further, feeling the tingles build as he paced behind me. With so many of my senses cut off, even the slight breeze each time he passed was evident, and it lit my skin with the submissive fire I'd grown to love.

The one I'd missed being hidden away at home for so long, sulking in my misery.

Then it came. The cane striking my ass. The whoosh of the cane, the sting and sound of it hitting my flesh, and Master pulled my hair hard. He hit me again, and again, and with each strike, I surrendered to him.

He knew I loved his cane. How safe it made me feel. So with each strike, he was showing me the mercy I'd hoped for.

I lost count at ten, but he kept going until wetness ran down my thighs. I wanted him to fuck me right there in front of everyone. I would have begged for it had my mouth not been full.

Master pulled me upright by my hair and turned me toward him. He slapped my cheek several times as well.

"You will obey and lift your arms."

My chest moved roughly again, and he wrapped his arms around me and told me I was safe. That he loved me. That I was *beautiful*.

As he lifted my dress a second time, I didn't fight him. I raised my arms high and as the dress left my body, something strange happened.

I felt no different than the last time I'd been naked in that room.

In fact, I felt exactly the same. Wet, submissive, and desperate for Master to humiliate me and make me come for everyone in the room. Nothing had changed but the bullshit I'd allowed to circle my mind.

The chatter didn't change either. Everyone sounded the same, and I heard no voices of condemnation or judgment. Not even gasps of shock as my missing breast and deep scars were suddenly on display for everyone there. At least ten people, maybe fifteen.

No one seemed to care. No one fled the room screaming at the monster about to be put on the cross.

Nothing made sense. Why had I been so worried? Felt so ashamed?

Then it hit me. The memory I'd suppressed earlier that day resurfaced, but this time it was easier to remember details as I had the safety of Master right next to me.

I pulled myself from my thoughts. I understood why it'd surfaced and there was no need to recall any more.

The shame that made me feel so heavy earlier began to lift. I'd been too hard on myself. I thought of the other women in the club. What if they'd been in my position? I realized I couldn't see them as less sexy. I saw them as *more* sexy, because scars mean pain, and for subs like me, pain means transcendence into something beautiful.

How could I have forgotten these things?

So much went through my head as Master moved me to the cross and faced me outward, toward everyone in the room. He secured my wrists and ankles to the cross with cuffs but left the one with the bells loose in case I needed to shake my wrist. The cool of the wooden cross pressed into my back and it reminded me of being put on display there. Of how good it felt to be Master's fucktoy and exhibitionist slave.

I was *his*, with consent and trust that he'd never once broken.

There wasn't much I could do to tell Master that I was feeling better, or that I'd figured out the problem, so I did the only thing I could in that moment. I stood as tall as possible and shoved my breast and lovely scar outward. The more I pushed forward, the stronger I felt inside.

Like fire, a phoenix rising... Not from ash, but from suffering.

Master ran his cane over my chest and I pushed outward even further, dropping into the sweetest place as I squirmed and ached for him.

He whacked me with his cane a few times and a rush of freedom pushed through me. Like more fire, but in my veins. I moaned through the gag, muffled and silenced with words, but my moans of ecstasy were clear.

"Good, girl!" Master shouted. I heard the pride in his voice. It made me let go even more and I moaned again.

Master's cane hit the floor and he passionately licked across my breast, then my missing breast. He traced my scar with his tongue while shoving three fingers inside my wet and ready cunt.

His thumb circled my clit as his fingers moved in and out. His tongue still moving between my breast and scar. The tingles between my legs were growing at an alarming rate and I wanted badly to plead—beg—for him to let me come like his little fucktoy. But I couldn't still.

So I squirmed and moaned as best I could.

I shoved my body forward and into him.

I whimpered, but this time, with desire and desperation.

"Does my girl want to come?"

"Mmmmhmmmm." I tried to speak, but gave up and nodded instead.

"What do good girls say?" His tone got firmer.

"Plllleeee," I tried to say, and Master removed his hand from me and unbuckled my gag.

He removed it, and my mask as well.

The moment I opened my eyes and saw everyone, my mouth fell open. There weren't just ten people there. The entire club was watching me. No one looked grossed out. Of the forty or so patrons, all looked just as entranced by my public display as they had before my surgery.

I looked at Master with surrender and gratitude in my eyes, and said, "Thank you, Master."

"For what?"

"For freeing me again."

Master caressed my cheek, his smile wide. *His* eyes were teary now. Though he didn't know of this new memory, Master was fully aware of my childhood trauma, so my words carried weight even without the new details. I sensed he was proud of me, and that made my heart warm.

"You're welcome, girl. It seems you've found your voice again." He moved directly in front of me. "Now beg, slut."

"Please let me come, Master?"

"Again!"

"Please, Master... Let me come?"

"Louder, slut!"

"Master, please! Please, may I come?"

He reached down and placed several fingers inside me again. Rougher this time, and I began to move into him without a conscious thought. His thumb circled my clit harder and faster, and he ordered me to look at my audience.

I obeyed.

The harder he fucked me with his hand, the more I pleaded for him to let me come. Until finally, he shouted, "Come, slut! Come hard for all these people!"

I obeyed again.

I came so hard I screamed. The orgasm ripped through me and consumed the pain and insecurities as it did. I knew who I was. I *loved* who I was.

I was an exhibitionist, beautiful, sexy, little fucktoy.

Master kept fucking me with his fingers and I kept coming. I released so hard that I eventually had to beg him to stop.

He laughed, but after a few, desperate pleas, he removed his fingers.

"Clean my fingers, slut."

Master held them to my mouth and I licked my own juices from them. Smelling and tasting what he'd made me do in front of all those people. I could do nothing but smile with everything in me as I gladly cleaned his fingers.

When I was finished, Master didn't let me off the cross just yet. Instead, he invited anyone up that wanted to tell me how beautiful or sexy I was. He let them touch and kiss my missing breast. And to my surprise, each touch and kiss felt like more fire. Even with my damaged tissue and loss of feeling in some areas.

I loved people loving my scar. Seeing it as beauty rather than a flaw. Something I'd always done with others but hadn't been able to overcome with myself until now.

I wanted to thank them for watching and giving me back my sense of self through their voyeurism, but I was still too deep. Still partially coming as some people touched me. It was amazing and I couldn't stop grinning.

Master waited for a while, standing next to me the entire time. But not in front. Not separating me from everyone else. Not *hiding* me.

Finally, he stepped between me and the others still lingering and took me down from the cross. He removed the cuffs and anklets, and then the bell bracelet, and helped me put my dress back on.

Part of me didn't want it on, but I knew I'd start shivering soon from all the adrenalin. Which meant clothing was vital. But I stood taller. I didn't lean into Master in the same desperate *hide me*, sort of way.

Finding myself again hadn't been hard. Maybe I'd not lost my confidence to begin with. I'd only thought I had.

It was then that I realized I didn't want the implant. I wanted to honor myself, and my body, *as is*. I wasn't less of a woman. I was a woman with a scar and a desperate desire to be put on display.

"Shall we go mingle?" Master asked.

"Yes, Master. But first, I've made up my mind about something."

"What's that, girl?"

"I don't want the implant." I smiled.

"I know," he said with an enormous smile of his own. "What are you, girl?"

"I'm a beautiful Goddess, Master."

"Good, girl."

Master held my cheeks and kissed me with a passion I'd not felt from him before. Then he took my arm and escorted me around the club.

The rest of the evening blurred as I caught up with friends, shared about my cancer and the choice to have my breast removed, about hating myself and not wanting to see anyone, and finally, about finding myself again. I thanked each and every one of them for being a part of that magical moment for me.

No one seemed angry that I'd shut them out, just thankful I was back.

By the time we arrived home that night, I'd hit a new level of tired. So much energy out and now I wanted nothing more than to cuddle up to Master and sleep. But first, I needed to take care of something...

I went to my room and retrieved my special bra, then took it to Master.

"Master, I'd like to donate this. Is that okay with you?"

"Of course, girl. Master is proud of you."

I set the bra on the table by the entryway and followed Master to bed. Satin sheets never felt so good as the coolness hit my sore skin. I snuggled into Master a different person. Someone more whole than I'd ever been with both my breasts. I now understood that what made me whole wasn't my body, my hair, my makeup or clothes, or even my breasts... What made me whole was embracing myself fully. Being me, without anything or anyone telling me who and what I was.

I was whole because I was *me*.

PUSHING BUTTONS
by Leandra Vane

Thanks to muscular dystrophy, both my life and body are the same shape: one gigantic question mark.

It's the shape I pulled myself out of at five every weekday morning. I sat on the bench in my shower as hot water pummeled my skin to a shade of bubblegum and my muscles relaxed into something I could work with.

The bangs on my pixie cut were long, but my hair was still a manageable length to wash and comb using my one good hand.

I took my time getting dressed. I wore the same kind of outfit every day: a sun dress with thigh high stockings underneath and a pair of black, knee high go-go boots that cover the brace I wore on my left leg. I pulled a necklace off the stand and slipped it on—my industrial art friend in college fashioned magnets onto all my necklace clasps so I could put them on myself. A cardigan went on to cover my twiggy arms—I owned the same sweater in three different colors.

I've found that when it comes to living in a body like

mine, you earn respect in the details. Which is why I wore a necklace every day and every dress I owned cinched at the waist. It's also why I stopped speaking.

Nothing killed respect faster than a dollop of saliva trailing down my chin if the word I tried to say happens to have a "T" in it. Or an "S" or an "F." Or most letters, really. On top of that, no one could understand me when I talked, anyway. My clumsy hands too spastic for sign language, I was left using text-to-speech apps and I was more than happy letting a machine speak for me. This way other people could fill in the blanks and color me in higher favor then they would if they could see how defective my body really was.

My purse was a miniature backpack with a 90's floral print. It was big enough to pack my lunch and hold my tablet, the device I used to talk to people, if I had to. The voice I chose was called Bridgette. She was good enough.

I was fairly certain we were in for some April Showers so I pulled on my fake leather jacket. I glanced at the rose gold cane leaning against the doorframe but I was feeling pretty good, so I left my apartment without it.

The bus stop was one block down from my apartment building. Twenty-three minutes later I arrived at work. I did data entry on real estate loans for a bank in a cubicle on the third floor. It wasn't where I thought a degree in writing would get me and I certainly didn't like my job. But where else could I go where I didn't have to hand out change, stand for long periods of time, or talk to anyone ever? Besides, they didn't care about my nose ring or the 14 hoops in my ears as long as I stayed in my cubicle. I'm fairly certain some of my co-workers came to work in their pajamas.

I always kept my headphones in my head through the bus ride and all the way to my desk to ward off any rogue small talk in the elevator.

Safely in my cubicle I set Bridgette up next to the phone and shoved my bag underneath the desk. I used the touch screen to get logged into the system. There was a new pack of unsharpened pencils and I took two out, pointing them eraser side down. This is how I typed most efficiently. Thus I went to town on the keyboard, dutifully entering figures into spreadsheets for the next eight hours of my day.

I disappeared until ten o'clock when my break time allowed me to surf recipe websites on my tablet for fifteen minutes. I had just found a promising chicken penne when she knocked.

"Hi! I'm Aly McCallister. I'm new. We're uh," she pointed to the cubicle behind her. "Neighbors. I've never worked in a cubicle before. Do you like it?"

This was all quite a lot at once. I made things even more awkward by having to close the internet on Bridgette and pull up the text-to-speech app.

I'm Chelsea Bleau.

Nice to meet you.

Cubicles steal your soul.

Aly's cherry red lips formed a surprised O for a moment, but just. "How long have you been working here?"

Too long.

Sorry.

Four years.

Aly smiled. "It's cool. I hear you. Well, I won't take up your break, but I wanted to say hi. Um. Maybe I'll see you again? When do you take lunch?"

12:15.

I eat in the break room on the second floor.

Because no one else does.

It's quiet.

We could talk there. She smiled and her whole body swayed forward. "Oh, cool, yeah! So. Um. Yeah. It's a date."

My fingers trembled around the pencil but I managed to type,

It's a date.

***

The break room on the second floor was indeed empty when I arrived for lunch. I set up Bridgette and fumbled about with my lunch. My heart was pounding and I had tunnel vision. I had no idea why I suggested we eat lunch together. After a near panic attack, I managed to get the lid off my tea bottle and my sandwich out of the bag. I concentrated on deep breathing as I armed myself with a butter knife and a stack of napkins.

I never ate in front of other people. It's why I never dated. I'd had one night stands, but no romantic dinners. I didn't mind fucking someone, but eating with someone else, that was too damn intimate.

Luckily, I had work lunches down to a science. I was always afraid someone would need to share the break room so I've practiced diligently to keep as much saliva and chewed up bits of food safely in my mouth. To achieve this, I had to eat very slowly and drink at exactly the right moment.

I cut my sandwich into half-inch by half-inch pieces. My bottle of tea would be the perfect ratio of sips between bites. I was still nervous so I took a couple extra napkins. Just in case.

I glanced at the clock. 12:23. I didn't know which would be worse: if I had to eat lunch in front of her or if she didn't show up at all.

I tapped my butter knife in contemplation. Why did I care so much if she didn't show up? Our conversation hadn't even lasted a full sixty seconds. I didn't know if she spelled Aly with a "y" or an "ie."

I didn't know her. But I was attracted to her.

Ever so brief as it was, our exchange had an easy attentiveness that was just... nice. But this was as far as my thoughts were allowed to wander as Aly rushed in.

"Sorry I'm late, I got lost coming back from the bathroom."

I was ready with my pencil eraser.

It's ok.

How's your first day going?

"Fuck me. I close my eyes and all I see are numbers."

You'll get used to it.

"I hope so. Sorry, I cuss a lot."

I don't mind.

She opened up her lunch box.

"I was running late this morning so I just grabbed." She pulled out a full size container of cottage cheese, an unopened bag of baby carrots, and a fork. She shrugged. "Good enough." I continued the conversation, keeping the topic safe.

Have you ever done data entry before?

"No. This job was pretty much a last minute thing. I just moved back home from Philadelphia to help take care of my mom—her health has really taken a turn for the worse. I needed a nine to five so I wouldn't be working weird hours or night shifts so I can be there when she needs me. This paid the best without being too stressful, so here I am."

I'm sorry about your mom.

"Me too. She's only 61. But, life, I guess."

What did you do in Philadelphia?

"I was just a waitress at a restaurant and lounge. Well, I guess technically I made it to assistant manager there."

Did you like it?

"Yeah, for the most part. We hosted a lot of events, like open mic nights for music or poetry. We even had a Burlesque night once a month."

Nothing that exciting here.

Besides, I don't think there's anyone here you would want to see do Burlesque.

"Who's that guy on the other side of you?"

Stewart.

"I bet he'd get freaky if we asked."

I'll leave the asking up to you.

She laughed, "I don't think you need to worry about that."

Do you miss Philadelphia?

"I do miss living in a bigger city. But I just went through a bad breakup. Well, not just, more like a year ago, so it's a good thing I finally got out of there. There are worse things than coming home." She ripped a hole open in the corner of the bag of carrots even though there was a zip-top.

"So, what do you do for fun around here?"

Most people leave around here when they want to have fun.

"Yeah, I bet. I'm scared to go out in case I run into someone I used to know in high school. Do you have friends around here to go out with?"

I don't go out much.

I'm a nerd and hang out online a lot.

"You do? I can give you my username, we could chat sometime."

I pulled up the messenger app I used the most on Bridgette and Aly entered her username.

"Cool. I'll add you when I get home tonight." She

crunched on a carrot. "I really like your dress."

Thank you.

"Where do you go shopping?"

Nowhere special.

Thrift stores, mostly.

"My kind of woman."

I like that.

I pressed the button for Bridgette to say those three words before I thought ahead to any socially awkward consequences of saying them. Luckily there were none as she smiled.

"I knew we were going to be friends when I saw the leather jacket on the back of your chair. I like thrifty rebels."

Before you know we'll be coordinating Burlesque shows at the water cooler.

"I guess I will have to talk to Stewart, then."

As lunch wended down to the last few minutes I expected Aly to ask about Bridgette or my pencils or my mountain of napkins or any number of things. But she did not. I found I had eaten my sandwich and drank all my tea without even realizing, not worried at all. After lunch I headed back to my desk with a smile and an image of Stewart in my mind that would not easily be eradicated.

***

A shiver darted down Nate's spine as James ran his fingers through Nate's long hair. Watching the professional veneer melt into wild abandon made Nate's knees shake with anticipation. Nate was coming unhinged himself but he managed to keep control long enough to dig in his fingernails and savor the feeling of James's firm cock as it slid—

***

Aly M: Hey what's up?

I stopped typing abruptly and nearly dropped one of my pencils as Aly's message popped onto my screen, obscuring the smut I had been writing.

I repositioned my pencils and typed,

Chelsea B: *Just taking it easy. How are you?*

Aly M: *Fine. Kind of want a drink. But I've settled for hot cocoa.*

Chelsea B: *I have vanilla chai tea myself.*

Aly M: *Never had it. Sounds amazeballs though.*

Chelsea B: *Never heard it called amazeballs before, but that description is fitting.* I made a mental note to put a couple bags of the tea in my purse to give to her the next day.

Aly M: *Sorry, I let go when no one is around to make me behave. AKA not at work.*

Chelsea B: *It's ok. I'm a lot different away from work, too.*

Aly M: *How so?*

I paused. I could have lied. But I didn't.

Chelsea B: *Well, I write erotica for one. It's gotten to be like a second job.*

Aly M: *What? Seriously? That's so cool!*

Chelsea B: *Amazeballs?*

Aly M: *Fuck yeah. What kind of erotica do you write? Really kinky stuff?*

Chelsea B: *Not so much kink, but things do get pretty dirty.*

Aly M: *Straight? Gay?*

Chelsea B: *Well, I write a lot of different pairings. Straight, same-sex. A few threesomes. One very special foursome.*

Aly M: *Is there a number when things officially become an orgy?*

Chelsea B: *Five, I think. I'd have to look it up though.*

Aly M: *Haha, awesome. So, are you, like, bi?*

I couldn't believe my pencils were typing the truth. I had never told anyone.

Chelsea B: *Yes, pretty sure.*

Aly M: *So, you know what you're writing about then ;)*

Chelsea B: *I'd like to think so.*

Aly M: *Do you sell a lot?*

Chelsea B: *I sell some. Not enough to ditch my career in data entry, though. Someday, maybe.*

Aly M: *That's awesome. I'd love to read some of your dirty writing.*

I quickly found a link and sent it.

Chelsea B: *Here's a story that's published online. It's an older one, but you'll get the idea.*

Aly M: *OMG thanks! Hey I g2g now but I will read this asap. Enjoy your tea.*

Chelsea B: *No problem. I will. Thanks.*

Aly M: *Night!*

Chelsea B: *Good night.*

Aly logged off and I sat for a minute looking at the little "offline" symbol next to her username. When the butterflies had eased I shook my head and pulled my story back up. Oh, yes. I had left Nate and James in quite a precarious situation.

***

Aly M: This one was my favorite by far. I really really really liked it.

Several weeks had passed and as requested I had been sending Aly dirty stories for her to read when she had a moment. She had offered great feedback on a few of my unpublished stories and was more than willing to tell me when she hated something. I was happy to see the latest offering had struck her fancy.

Chelsea B: *Thanks. I'm glad you enjoyed.*

Aly M: *If that's what you can do with words, I'd love to see what you can do in person.*

Chelsea B: *Not much. That's why I write.*

Aly M: *Oh, I don't know...*

I didn't know what to say so I just waited for her to type something.

After a minute she did.

Aly M: *So. Guess what?*

Chelsea B: *Umm... What?*

Aly M: *I liked the buttons on your dress today.*

Chelsea B: *Haha, thanks.*

Aly M: *Every time I walked by your desk I was very distracted by your buttons.*

Chelsea B: *They are fake buttons so*—I stopped typing. *Delete, delete, delete.*

Why were you so distracted by my buttons?

Aly M: *I wanted to undo them.*

One

By

One.

Chelsea B: *...I'm not sure you would like what you find beneath my buttons.*

Aly M: *I think I would really, really like what I would find underneath your buttons. I've fantasized about it, but... I want to know.*

I hesitated, my mind churning between heaven and hell. She liked me. Like that. And what did I have to offer her? My silence caused her to type,

Aly M: *I'm really sorry. If you don't like me like that. I hope I didn't just fuck up our friendship.*

Chelsea B: *No, you didn't. I just don't see how you would like me. Like that.*

Aly M: *Are you joking? I liked you from the second I saw you, this awesome punk rock chick with those boots and that hair. And you were just so cool to me even though I was a fucking hot mess. And then your stories. Fuck. Chelsea. I want you. I want to be a part of your*

story.

Chelsea B: *Well... you can start by undoing my buttons.*

Aly M: *What?*

Chelsea B: *Start with the top button and tell me what happens.*

Aly M: *...I start at the top, my fingers trembling around the pearl finish. With each button your dress loosens inch by inch until the fabric falls away.*

Chelsea B: *I feel the rush of cool sweep over my back, followed by your gentle caress. My body is twisted, contorted, tense.*

Aly M: *My hands begin to massage your shoulders, your muscles start relaxing beneath my touch. I rub lower and knead my thumbs into the small of your back.*

Chelsea B: *I lean into you, your forceful but gentle hands melting the pain away. I grasp your wrists and invite your fingertips to tease the band of my panties.*

Aly M: *I hesitate for a moment to feel your body respond with anticipation, your hips thrust forward so slightly as I dig my fingertips into your hip bones.*

Chelsea B: *We continue this erotic dance and an aching throb begins to pulse just below my navel.*

Aly M: *I push my hand inside and your heat burns into my fingertips.*

Chelsea B: *I rock into your hand, your fingers venturing over my pussy lips, spreading them apart and slipping just a few centimeters inside. A flicker of heat shoots between my legs and my wetness slicks your* *fingertips.*

Aly M: *I reach with my other hand to pull your panties down around your hips. I want you exposed to me, your round ass curves deliciously and your panties fall to your ankles.*

Chelsea B: *You reach up and run your fingers through my hair, nicely at first, but then you grip a fistful of my hair and pull back. I moan and give in, like chocolate melting on your tongue.*

Aly M: *With one hand still stroking your wet pussy I bend you over the desk and thrust with my hips. You are already wet, but I want you wetter. I have a surprise.*

Chelsea B: *I whimper beneath your force, my tits smashed into the table top, my pussy trembling as you pull your hand away. I wait nicely for your surprise.*

Aly M: *Pink or green?*

Chelsea B: *Hmm. Green.*

Aly M: *Good choice. I pull out a green vibrator, and take a moment to appreciate how much I will enjoy fucking you with it.*

Chelsea B: *I breathe deep and take a moment to appreciate how much I will like being fucked.*

Aly M: *I rub the head against your labia, wetting it with your juices. I turn the vibrator onto the lowest setting and push the rumbling toy into you.*

Chelsea B: *My body spasms hungrily around it. I bob against your thrusts to take the vibrator deeper inside.*

Aly M: *After you get comfortable, I twist the knob and the pulsing vibration doubles in intensity. I hold* *fast, my wrist aching as I fuck you hard.*

Chelsea B: *I moan low and loud rocking in time to your force. I beg you to fuck me harder as I quiver on the verge of climax.*

Aly M: *I reach around with my free hand and drive my fingers under your bra, squeezing your tit as hard as I can.*

Chelsea B: *The touch sends me over the edge and I come writhing over the desk as you clutch my body close.*

Aly M: *I pull the vibrator from you, watching the juices drip from my neon green toy.*

Chelsea B: *I won't let it end at that. Before you get away I turn and kiss you, nudging my tongue inside, gently at first but a fiercer mood takes hold. I tear your shirt open, the buttons flying everywhere. I pull your bra down revealing your hard nipples and ample breasts.*

Aly M: *I gasp into your greedy mouth and await your caress. (My nipples are pierced.)*

Chelsea B: *I dip my head to suck your left nipple and hold the piercing between my teeth like a sweet, hard candy.*

Aly M: *I moan and pull you close to me, wanting to feel you everywhere, always.*

Chelsea B: *A trail of saliva gleams down your swollen nipple, your breast peppered with the crescent moons of teeth marks.*

Aly M: *I beg you to take me, be dirty with me, be kinky and take me.*

Chelsea B: *I shove you away from me, from my kisses, from my touch. I want you to know what it feels like to be bent over my desk. I push you down and put my fist in your hair. I reach around and undo your pants. Before you can protest I pull your pants and panties to your knees exposing your bare ass. I bend you further to admire your aroused pussy, already wet for me.*

Aly M: *I beg you to take me, please. Please.*

Chelsea B: *I slip two fingers inside and revel in the searing heat. You invite me in and I pulse my touch as deep as I can.*

Aly M: *Yes, yes!*

Chelsea B: *But I stop, suddenly and pull away. You shudder for a moment and I leave you to wait.*

Aly M: *No! Why! Please!*

Chelsea B: *When I am satisfied that you are desperate for release I pull my hand back and slap you across your ass.*

Aly M: *Oh god, yes.*

Chelsea B: *Your whole body jerks to attention and I spank you again, three, four, five times. Your flesh darkens with the blushing pink of arousal.*

Aly M: *Yes, harder, please.*

Chelsea B: *I release your hair, knowing I don't have to hold you down—you beg for my open palm, your mint painted fingernails clawing the slick surface of the desk in surrender.*

Aly M: *Fuck, I'm going to come.*

Chelsea B: *I encourage your orgasm with each full,*

hard snap on your skin and swim in the moans of your ecstasy and the uncontrolled thrusts of your hips.

Aly M: *Dedfrghjkhl.ki321x o.;oknjbhvgc*

I leaned back in my computer chair and let the wave of orgasm flow through my shaking body, the hot liquid soothing my tense limbs, transforming pain into bliss. I was wet and trembling and drenched in sweat. Everything had been messy and obscene and magical and who the fuck cared where she pulled that vibrator from and oh so perfectly perfect. When I resurfaced from my pleasure, Aly had typed,

Aly M: *Wow. Just wow. That was seriously hot. And nice. And hot. And naughty and amazing.*

Chelsea B: *Amazeballs.*

Aly M: *Fuck yeah. Uh, let's do that again sometime.*

Chelsea B: *Considering all my dresses have buttons I'm sure we will.*

Aly M: *Oh, God. How will we get on without Stewart hearing?*

Chelsea B: *Aw, let him.*

Aly M: *I'm so happy we met.*

Chelsea B: *Me too. You're the first person in a very long time who I feel like I can be myself around. But I'm still a little scared.*

Aly M: *So am I. My last relationship messed me up. But I'm willing to try. I want to be myself too.*

Chelsea B: *We can take things slow. But tonight meant a lot to me. Thank you.*

Aly M: *I can't wait to see where this goes.*

Chelsea B: *Me too. At this rate I'll have plenty of new story ideas. I have a feeling you'll be a part of every one from now on.*

Aly M: *OMG, I'm smiling so much right now.*

Chelsea B: *Me too.*

That was the truth. I was smiling, without fear or shame. The truth was also that I didn't know where our relationship would go from here. But I did know, for the first time in my life, my whole body and life felt like a joyous, eager exclamation point.

INSIDE OUT
by Anna Sky

We're sat in front of the television in our pyjamas when he works his hand into my hair. My body tenses in response to his tight grip and I can't turn to face him as he speaks. "I think we need to go upstairs, don't we?" His voice is low, and I don't say anything; I don't need to.

I let him guide me from the sofa, up on to my feet, both of us waiting to see what my balance does. His grip never slackens, tugging just hard enough on the roots of my hair to slow me down. He propels me from behind, checking that my body is strong enough for his games.

And then he's on me. Backing me hard into the doorframe, pulling my hands up above my head and snaking a hand round my throat. He pushes my legs apart, forcing me against the cold wood, and leans into me. His cock bulges through his cotton bottoms, pushing hard into my belly. I barely notice; I have other distractions.

The feel of his grip on my throat alone is enough that time slows and I become heavy-eyed at his mercy. My limbs, leaden before we started, now no longer belong to me and without his support, I think I'd slide to the ground.

He kisses me, tongue pushing roughly into my mouth. I open to accommodate him, obedient and willing. He is not gentle, taking what he wants of me and I want him to. I want him to have every little piece of me; I know that by the time he's finished, I will be rebuilt, stronger. Still cherished. Still adored. There's a price to get there, but I'm more than willing to pay it.

His hard thigh pushes against my crotch, pinning me to the frame, building the need in me and he pulls back from the kiss. "You're mine, aren't you?"

I don't answer, letting his words dance across my skin, working their way deep into every pore until I'm sure he's branded me.

"Answer me," he growls, hot breath on my cheek and I nod. "Good girl," he replies and works his hand into the back of my hair again.

He guides me from the doorway to the bottom stair. And pushes me down to my hands and knees. In my time-slowed state, I smile. He knows I found the stairs challenging today and he's let my health become part of our game. Every time we play, he manages to dominate me without my limitations getting in our way and we both thrive on it.

I start crawling one tread at a time and I know he'll let me take as long as I need, waiting patiently. He's safe in the knowledge I wouldn't dare slow out of disobedience. We're both far too aware of the consequences for that. I know too, that he's watching my bottom wiggle as I move up each step, my pyjama shorts only just covering the swell of my arse.

I'm at the top when he tells me to kneel and wait. I settle, his hand brushing over my shoulder as he passes me and walks into our bedroom. When he returns, the glint in his eye and set of his jaw tells me he has a plan. This could have been an impromptu thing—perhaps a spanking or a no-mercy fucking. But his face tells a different story.

He holds up a blindfold. It slips straight on, soft leather on the outside pulling around the contours of my face. On the inside, a fur lining sits against my eyes and the bridge of my nose, cutting out all the light. He needs a lot of light to see and the brightness is often too much for me. It's too much sensory input when I'm breathing hard to process the beautiful pain he inflicts.

The blindfold works for us both and I love how vulnerable it makes me feel. A nervous anticipation runs through me from head to toe and I try not to shiver, instead focusing on my breath.

I don't know how long he stands watching me but I'm relieved that it only seems a short burst of time. The blindfold does funny things to my perception of time removing all visual clues. He takes each of my wrists in turn, stroking up and down my forearms to loosen off the muscle before strapping on cuffs. These don't allow me much movement. The firmness of the wide leather bands holds me in place so I can't escape. I don't even try any more.

I take a few deep breaths to centre myself. If he's cuffing me, he's planning on hurting me in the most beautiful and creative of ways. The restraint means I'll be powerless to resist. I become aware of a dull throb in my cunt at the idea of it, my nipples hardening. This is what I want, no, what I need.

He guides my hands behind my back, massaging my shoulders to ease the muscle. The hard metallic snap of a trigger hook cuts across the silence. It clips my hands together so my body is now at his command. He's at my elbow, helping me scramble to my feet. As I stand, I stretch out my legs, not wanting cramp and pain to interfere with his plans.

He pulls me towards the bedroom, a quick tug on my upper arm to make me follow. I stop when his hands are on my shoulders, fingertips gripping hard into the tops of my arms.

"You're going to let me do what I want." It was a statement, not a question, and I nod in affirmation. "You're my little fucktoy tonight and I expect you to behave."

The pounding in my cunt steps up a notch. His words wind round me, my cheeks flaming with the shame of his hold over me. We both know I can stop this game at any time and we both know I won't.

He roughly forces my chin up, so our eyes would meet were it not for the blindfold. His hand drops down the taut skin on my throat, inch by slow inch, until it rests against my collar bone. It tightens; if I weren't completely pliable before, he's just assured my complete submission.

I moan. It's the only sound to have escaped my lips since he pulled me off the sofa and it surprises me, loud in my ears and deeper than I expected.

I moan again when his other hand presses against my cunt, his fingers roughly grabbing and pinching at my pussy. The fabric of my shorts is rough against me as he gropes. He's never gentle when we play, but my body doesn't react well to gentle. I used to fantasise about soft butterfly kisses and fingertips trailing over my skin. In reality, it turns me hypersensitive and leaves me nauseated. He learnt early on that firm and rough work so much better for us both.

He pinches at me again before pulling the waistband of my shorts. The seam see-saws between my pussy lips, chafes against my clit in delicious strokes. I moan again, and again when he pinches my nipple, holding it in a mean grasp. He plays me like a musical instrument. A litany of moans and groans escape me every time he pinches, squeezes, pokes, pulls. I sink deeper into my headspace.

And then he throws me back onto the bed, a sudden, unexpected movement. It knocks all the air out of my lungs, silencing me. He's centred me, face-down, exactly where he wants, no limbs hanging off that could ache or cause my joints to spasm. He spends a moment shuffling the pillows and duvet. Checking in with me that I'm not in discomfort with any rucks or folds. It's the minor details to prevent my sensory overload, having to call my safewords.

He rests his hand on the back of my neck, holding my face down into the covers so it's hard to breath. His fingers are firm, warm against me. And then he releases me, another reminder I'm subject to his every whim. I turn my head to the side, taking a deep and grateful breath of air. Time seemed slippery and thick before; it's even harder to grasp now. I give in to it, letting myself drift further into subspace. It's where my body feels light and bright, how I think it used to, though it's hard to remember. When I'm there, I float and fly; my brain slows, tension leaves my body and I just exist in the moment. In an intoxicating, blissful endorphin-fuelled haze.

He unclips my wrists and refastens them to the headboard above. Lifting my hips, he peels off my shorts. I shudder in pleasure as he massages the length of my legs to straighten and spread my legs. His hands squeeze and pinch as they move down. I hear a clink as he picks up the cuffs and then warm leather encases my ankles. A tug on each leg lets me know I'm attached to the foot of the bed. I'm now helpless and unable to move and a cold shiver passes through me. I'm holding my breath, waiting for that first touch or strike wherever it may land.

The mattress moves either side of me. In my mind

he's poised over me on the bed, contemplating my curves and demeanour. I've seen the look on his face before. His eyes blaze with an intensity as he sinks into his headspace, like he's about to devour me. Something touches my cheek, surprising me. He caresses me with it, trailing it across my jaw and down my neck. It's pliable enough that I think it's the riding crop and hold my breath again, tensing. He passes it over my right breast and with a quick flick, taps it harder just below my nipple. I jerk in response. It's not painful, but unexpected. I was right about it being the crop.

His merciless exploration of my body continues. The crop's firm tip probes and tickles as it nudges over every inch of my chest and stomach. I wriggle and he presses his toes into the fleshy part of my belly, holding me still: a warning. His toes edge down until they're pressing into my mons and I impulsively thrust my hips up into them. He laughs as he pulls his foot away. "Not yet," he says and I know I'm pouting, instinct taking over again. I hope he doesn't see it as an excuse for making me work harder for my release. The tip of the crop trails a random path down the inside of my thigh and I exhale, releasing nervous energy.

He strikes the inside of my thighs with the crop. It's gentle, not-quite-painful and I find myself pacing my breath to his rhythm. Several taps and I breath in. Several taps more and I breathe out. In, out, in, out, in, out. I am counting in my head, anticipating the beat. He hits harder, maintaining the pace and my inner thighs start to throb. Each tap brings a jolt of pain, enough that it stings on impact. Not too much that I can't bear it. The bite from each strike doesn't fully recede before I receive the next one. I breathe harder, still the same rhythm, I'm still matching his pace.

When he stops, my thighs are throbbing hard, but I miss him building more layers of pain. It makes me feel strong and able to take what he hands out. It's the beginning of an endorphin cocktail, the high that I'm after. Every strike takes me further out of my head and deeper into subspace. I hope it won't be long before he lets me sink into its welcoming depths. I'm so close.

The crop moves to my pussy, and muscle-memory makes me wince. My brain hates what he's about to do but my traitorous body welcomes it. The crop strikes, hard enough for me to tense and I exhale a full breath in jerky, ragged doses. He waits for me to recompose myself and relax before he snaps the crop again. It hurts so good. Sharp strikes of pain flash through me and my clit pulses in response. I want more, another, and try to ignore my brain yelling how much I hate it. Another flash and another; he's enjoying my conflicted reaction enough to carry on.

He only stops when I start shivering; it's a warning to us both that I'm close to overload. The bed shifts round me and he's at my side, changing his methods to something I can manage. He scratches his nails methodically up and down me, gripping my neck, pinching, squeezing. He's at my thighs, my pussy, my belly. He knows how to keep me from surfacing, and I'm grateful; he understands my needs. Guttural moans and groans escape me and I know they please him. We both have desires that need re-affirming.

He eases off and unclips the cuffs from the bed, massaging my wrists and ankles to relax the muscles. I draw my limbs back to myself feeling light and airy and roll to face him.

"I'm taking off the blindfold," he whispers and I nod, bringing my hands up to my face. The tightness around my eyes loosens and I hold the darkness in place for a few moments more. Slowly, I move it away allowing my vision to re-adjust. I blink into the light and realise he's smiling at me. I try to smile back but everything is slow and hazy and I don't know whether I've succeeded.

He pulls the big support cushion out from under the bed. I know I've only had a brief reprieve and now must ready myself for round two. He settles it in the middle of the bed and pats it with his hand, beckoning me over. I swing my body round and shuffle myself over its bulk on all fours. My hips push into its apex and my bottom is in the air, my torso supported. He pushes me harder into the cushion and it forces my head down towards the duvet. I feel a sudden stab of vulnerability.

He runs his fingers through my hair, it's calming and I feel grounded, ready for more. He clips both my ankles together and does the same with my wrists. I can't wriggle far now and my body pulses in nervous anticipation.

I breathe again, some of the treacle-time has lifted in our interlude and I'm in control of myself again. He leans and kisses my forehead. "Good girl," he whispers. A thrill runs through me; his words are powerful.

He disappears from my line of sight and rests his hand in the small of my back. It's warm and comforting and the pounding in my clit grows stronger. I know what he's going to do next. His other hand comes down on my bottom. Over and over. He cups his palm and it sounds hollow as it strikes, landing as a deep thud. He covers the whole of my bottom in easy strokes moving down the backs of my thighs.

Slap. Throb. Slap. My body responds to his rhythm. It rushes through me, roaring in my ears, pounding in my clit. I am moving and moaning, barely aware of myself.

He spanks harder and harder; the blows should be an effort for him too. The cushion absorbs some of the power of the spanks as they shudder through me but they're still huge hits. They should bring tears to my eyes and make me beg him to stop, but I don't. I'm too far gone. When it feels this good, he can't really hurt me.

I hear him now, over the sound of my moans and his slaps. "You're my beautiful whore aren't you? My slut, my princess."

His words wash through me, elevating me. They should be words of shame and degradation but they're not. They're words of worship and adoration. I get off to this; the way he reduces me to this state yet all I do is fly higher.

"You deserve this."

Yes, I do.

"And you'll take it for me."

Yes, I will.

"You're a filthy, dirty girl. My filthy, dirty girl."

My heart fills with pride and I want to explode.

He slows to a stop and I push back into his hand, instinct taking over once more. He laughs, a low chuckle that bursts out of him with no warning. I think he's found his Dom space.

He moves again, pressing his body up against my bottom and thighs. He rakes his fingertips down my back and repeats, this time digging in his nails. I shudder. Parallel scratches deepening the further down my spine. I squirm under him, pushing down into the cushion but I'm trapped. He's etching his ownership of my body onto me; thick red lines that will take days to fade. The spanking was a manageable sensation but the scratching takes me to a different place. It's sting, it's solid edges of pain and I have to fight it, stop it from taking over me.

His fingers trail down to my bottom, pinching. It hurts; my spanked flesh is sore and I cry out. He pinches harder, taking pleasure in my pain, digging his fingers in wherever he can. I turn into one long, slow moan, desperate for him to stop yet never wanting him to.

He moves his hands to knead my shoulders, rolling the muscles hard between finger and thumb. I try to move away but I can't escape. Instead I sink back and feel the warmth from his thighs on the back of mine.

He works a hand up into my hair again and pulls his other hand down my back. This time, his fingertips drag, no nails bite in. They are firm and strong against my flesh but I no longer have to fight against the edge of pain. "Are you wet?" he murmurs, snaking his hand between my thighs. I'm embarrassed that pain takes me to this place and my cheeks flare in shame. We both know he needn't ask.

He dances his fingers across my pussy, probing and pushing until he slides them deep into me. I moan and try to arch back against them but his hand in my hair holds me tight. He laughs and continues to tease me.

Shivers of pleasure pulse through me from head to toe. At my core, my clit is swollen and needy, the pulse and pounding in it adding to the rhythm he's already coaxed out of me. I soften, swaying to my internal music, releasing moans and purrs of pleasure. He strokes his fingers over me again and again, coating them in my juices and sliding them in and out of me a fraction at a time.

With the little movement I have, I squirm to get the most pressure from his fingers. He feels so good, it's too little and too much at the same time. I don't want him to stop but don't know how much more I can take. I want him to make me explode. He will, I know he will, but I know he's enjoying bringing me ever closer to the edge right now. It's almost like he's daring himself to bring me ever-closer without letting me come... game over.

He shuffles behind me, thighs wrapping round mine

to let his cock nudge my wet folds. He leans over, his mouth near my ear. "I'm going to fuck you now. I'll take my time, make you wait." Whether it's the effect of his words or his voice, my entire cunt spasms in desperate anticipation. I'm so swollen and desperate for release but I can't tell him. My voice is lost in the abyss of pleasure-pain where I'm happily floating.

His fingertips grip hard into my thighs and he drives his cock into me. I feel the bruising imprint of every digit digging into my flesh and a sleepy smile spreads over my face. He's using me in just the way I love. I feel wanted, worshipped and alive. The whole bed rocks as he pistons in and out, over and over. The head of his dick hits against my cervix with every inward thrust. It's overwhelming and painful but still I greedily want more, harder, deeper. I don't tense at it; I'm too deep in my head.

Each time he withdraws I miss his girth, his pressure and warmth on my thighs. My body is so soft and relaxed all I can do is let him take his pleasure from me. Words form in my head but I can't vocalise them. Other than the noises that inadvertently escape me, I am engulfed in a silence. It's a beautiful thing. I let go of everything; my head is empty, devoid of thought and I collapse in on myself, my world shrinking to just him and me in the moment.

Behind me the thrusting stops and I hear guttural grunt from him as he comes hard. His fingers dig in, grasping and scratching as he peaks. Layers on top of layers of sensation anchoring me deep.

He pulls away to unfasten my bonds and manoeuvres me so I'm lying on my back. His hands briefly massage up and down my arms and legs as I stretch out, my limbs grateful for their release. In my hazy state, I grin at him and he leans down, pushing his lips against mine.

His tongue thrusts into my mouth, taking me by surprise and it takes me a moment to respond. His hand is already roaming across my belly and thighs, circling in tiny movements around my mons and pounding clit. Every time I thrust into his hand he moves it away; breaking off his kiss to grin at me. He slows until his hand is resting on my pussy, brushing against me with the lightest of touches.

He slides his middle finger down between my lips, the merest of sensations but it's just enough to take me to the edge. He circles the pad of his finger against me, deliberately maintaining too gentle a stroke for me to find relief. My cunt is aching for release and I don't know how much longer I can bear his torture. I can't come yet he won't let me come down either.

He brings his mouth down and bites the underside of my breast. In the same moment, he grabs my pussy in his hand, pinching hard, finally giving me the pressure I crave. I convulse into his palm, wave after wave of intensity ripping through my body with unexpected force. My whole body shakes and shudders, tensing and releasing over and over. It's an echo of the strength of the contractions inside. He holds on to me, pressing me to the bed and the roaring slows gradually to a murmur, letting me catch my breath.

I lie back and the room slides back into focus. I start to notice details; the red heat of my buttocks, the throb of the marks on my thighs. Unthinking, I curl into a ball - the shivers are threatening to take me over. It's the start of the come down and he wraps me tight in a blanket. I am safe and protected.

He strokes my hair in long, slow, comforting movements. "Good girl," he whispers and manoeuvres behind me until I'm spooned in his arms. The warmth from his body soaks into me and I greedily take his heat. Until know, I didn't know I was cold. I realise I'm purring, it's the only noise in the room. My voice hasn't returned to me yet, I'm still in my head but it doesn't matter. Our familiarity with each other means words aren't needed.

Wrapped in my cocoon, I bask in the silence. My limbs feel loose and relaxed and I'm full of contentment. My Dom knows me and my limits so much better than I know myself. He knows me inside out.

IN REAL LIFE
by Janine Ashbless

'No one should be alone for New Year,' he said. 'We could meet up, if you wanted.'

So I've agreed to meet Bryn in a railway station. A neutral public place with plenty of people around, just like they tell you. I'm not stupid. I've travelled all over the world, including countries where women are presumed fair game if they don't have their hair covered, or if they wear shorts. But in actuality this warrants more caution, here in my own country—where the rules are slacker and the men more likely to break them.

I'm on a train, going to meet a man I've only known through the Internet. For a date, sort of. 'Nothing heavy,' he promised. 'No expectations. We might hate each other on sight, after all.'

I've known Bryn online for eight months now, while I've been working in all sorts of countries and he's been sat at his desk back in England. He's an IT geek and he works from home. His life is lived in the virtual world, and that's where we met. That's where I go to find familiar friends for a couple of hours a night, after pitching up in yet another strange town and another identikit hotel.

Me? I'm more boring than you'd think, from looking at my passport. I'm an auditor. I work for a public quango, checking up that the money charities get is really being spent in the field on what they say it is. I enjoy the job, and the travelling, but I like to have somewhere I can go to get away from it all. My haven is a virtual one.

I met Bryn in *Second Life*. He was busy building a functioning orrery when I saw him first—he's that sort of a guy—and he looked like a pitch-black hermaphrodite with a starscape mapped all over his body and spiral galaxies for eyes. His avatar name is Pelagic Walker. His real name, he eventually revealed, was Bryn Evans. I wonder if he'll have a Welsh accent.

He says he's single. He says a thousand things about himself which may or may not be true. It's far too easy to lie online; to want your real life to live up to the flawless virtual version. But I have been careful. I haven't told him my surname and he doesn't know where I live when I'm in the UK. I did send him a photo—me sitting on a sun-bleached hillside, grinning into the distance—but I'm wearing opaque shades and a hat and all you can really work out is that I'm blonde and tanned and rangy. I want to be able to walk anonymously away if I don't like what I see. He did send me some photos of himself and he's pretty good-looking in those. I've looked him up using every search engine I can think of. So far there haven't been any warning signs.

Well, except the time I suggested we voice chat. He said he stuck to IMing. No further discussion. That's a little weird.

We've spent hours swapping messages and we're firm friends, in the virtual world. He's funny and acerbic and a bit cynical. His messages are almost always spelled out in full English, so I figure him for a bit anal. He takes my complaints about work in his stride, he asks smart questions about the places I've been to, and he doesn't pry into my personal life. Although he knows some stuff, of course. He knows I'm good at being on my own, he knows I love limes and the smell of rain on dust and having my back rubbed. That I hate cotton-wool and can't eat fish. He knows I'm single and not looking for a serious relationship.

Not interested. I've had too many boyfriends flake under the pressure of having me away for weeks at a time. They all end up getting hysterically jealous or just so bored that they screw someone more attainable behind my back. Bollocks to the lot of them; a long-distance relationship is more trouble than it's worth. Which makes it ironic that I'm standing in the aisle of a train carriage, watching a city railway station slide into place around me. His train should have got into town this morning, according to his last message. We're supposed to meet under the big Victorian clock.

This is where, I tell myself, I find out whether he's

the guy in his picture or a fat balding bloke in his fifties with corduroy trousers and clammy hands. Which'll be bloody awkward, frankly, because we've had sex already. Cybering, you know. Avatars bumping pixels. Me and him in our own rooms, each with one hand down our pants, typing frantically with the other and getting increasingly more incoherent as self-control breaks down:

> *I'm wriggling on your lap Bryn, rubbing up against your cock.*

> *I'm so hard, Ellie, hard like rock.*

> *Big too.*

> *Huge. And getting bigger every second. You're going to need to be wet for what I've got to give you.*

> *then it's a good thing my panties are soaked thru already. i'm so wet it's running out of me.*

> *I pull your panties down. They're tight around your thighs and I'm so impatient I have to rip them.*

> *OMG yes!*

> *I want you, Ellie. I want your tight wet pussy around my big cock. It's so hard now it's throbbing.*

> *i want you too. i need you inside me, bryn. i need your cock in my pussy.*

> *I'm sticking it deep into you now. Now.*

> *oh god I'm nearly ready to come already it feels so good!*

> *Slowly to start with...*

> *fuck me!!*

> *Yes I'm fucking you. Fucking you hard.*

Yeah, not exactly Shakespeare. But fun. We do it quite a lot. It certainly helps pass the time in a hotel room with nothing but foreign pop channels to watch.

Oh hell, I hope he's not lied to me.

It's not a date, not really. But there is a possibility, all our protests notwithstanding. A question hanging over us: *Will We?* I brought condoms, just in case. The online sex has been so good and I can't help the anticipation that makes my heart thump as I step down onto the platform. I can't help the clench and flutter of my pussy, or the way my awareness keeps being drawn to the rub of my nipples against my clothes. I heft my little knapsack and wet my lips, pushing my shoulders back as I walk slowly toward the clock tower.

And there he is. Holy shit. Just like his photos—but tall. I wasn't expecting tall. Dark hair on his scalp and jaw cropped to a uniform fuzz. Big, dark, warm eyes, looking a bit anxious. Oh, yes—it's the eyes that draw you to that face. He's hot, no argument. I catch his gaze and the word pops out of my mouth before I have time to consider any further, my mind made up without bothering to tell me, it seems: 'Bryn?'

His expression lights up and he comes forward and takes both my hands, stooping to kiss my cheek. The prickle of his stubble seems to wake me from an inner dream.

'Wow—it's so strange to see you for real,' I gush.

We're both grinning at each other. Gently he takes my arm and leads me toward the clock, and I'm still in the first shock of wondering what I should be saying and just starting to wonder why he hasn't said anything himself, when I see there's a second man. A man who's been waiting there with Bryn. He's shorter and slighter with sandy hair that stands up in tufts, and sharp twinkly eyes. He makes me think of Hobbits.

'Ellie?' he says. 'Hi. I'm Hugh.'

'Uh. Hi.' My eyes cut to Bryn. What's going on?

Bryn's let go of my arm; now his hands lift and move, dancing through a series of gestures. Hugh watches, before speaking to me.

'I'm his interpreter. He says, "I'm sorry, I hope it's not too much of a surprise."'

Some hope. My jaw drops. 'Oh,' I manage to mew.

'How was your journey?'

'Fine. Just fine. No problem. Um.' My brain is freewheeling, the gears slack no matter how hard I pedal.

'Our train was packed. People coming in for the sales, I guess.'

'Why didn't he tell me?' I blurt.

Hugh frowns slightly. 'You should look at Bryn if you're talking to him. Keep eye contact. It helps him lip-read.'

The realisation of just how rude my last utterance was crashes in on me, and I go scarlet as I turn back to Bryn. 'Oh. Oh. Right. I'm sorry! But—why didn't you tell me?'

He shrugs ruefully, then signs. He has long dark hands, I notice, remembering some of the places the virtual versions of those fingers have been, and the things they've done to me.

'He says that he would, but he thought you might not come. Some people say they aren't bothered, but then they lose their nerve and don't turn up.'

'Oh crap.' I'm not sure whether I'm ashamed for him or for me. 'Of course I'd have come, Bryn.'

He smiles.

'Great,' says Hugh, fishing a packet of cigarettes out of his pocket and adding, 'I can't light up in here, can I?' Signing one-handed, he asks us both, 'So, what's the plan? Where are we going?'

'You're coming with us?' This time I am talking to him. Hugh looks nonplussed.

'D'you know BSL?'

'No.'

'Then you probably need me.'

'On a date?'

He looks slightly startled. 'He didn't say it was a date.' Then he flashes me a look of approval that's not the least bit platonic. 'The lucky bugger.'

As he turns to Bryn and they exchange a flurry of gestures I mumble, 'No, well, it's not really, not a proper date.' But there's no way of telling if either man has noticed.

'I'm happy playing gooseberry,' is Hugh's verdict, 'but he asks if it's okay with you. I mean, I'll bugger off anytime you guys want me to.'

'Uh... It's okay.' God knows I need an interpreter. The alternative is the two of us finding an Internet cafe and IMing each until we've broken the ice. Which seems a little too cowardly, really. I catch Bryn's eye and ask, 'Where shall we go first?'

***

Bryn takes us to a restaurant—Italian, nice but not fancy—for an early dinner. By the time we're onto our coffees I've largely got the hang of the three-way conversation. I feel self-conscious; it's horribly easy for me to look away or cover my mouth or to interrupt without thinking. What's most difficult is reconciling the Bryn in my head, the one I know online, with the man sitting in front of me. Online Bryn is quick and confident and cerebral, his personality defined by words. This Bryn is wholly physical, and distractingly so: there's a fuzz of dark hair on his forearms and I find myself wondering, in the pauses, whether he'll have a mat of hair on his chest too, whether his thighs and belly will be furred. He's good-looking enough for my curiosity to be more than idle—but my horniness embarrasses me and makes me more awkward. Conversation through our intermediary is so much slower and Bryn comes across as almost shy—not the man I know at all. I wonder if I'm missing nuances and details because I can't sign. In fact I'm sure I am; there are expressive gestures that come out sounding flat as Hugh interprets, jokes that

Hugh laughs at but doesn't pass on to me. I ache to communicate with Bryn as we do online. We can't even really discuss Second Life because Hugh isn't a participant and I feel bad about excluding him because it turns out that he and Bryn are old friends. The two of them met at their local Deaf Club. Hugh's family all sign because his younger sister is deaf.

It's only when we go out into the dark evening, and it turns out that my date has booked tickets for the ice-skating rink that's been set up in the park, that I learn to let go of my mental Bryn and enjoy the company of the one here. It's years since I've worn skates and I'm all over the place, wobbling and falling; it's a good job I've got both men there to catch me. There's no particular need for conversation as we laugh and yelp and collide with each other, and all my concentration goes on keeping my feet under me. By the time our hour is up I'm really enjoying myself. Enjoying the company of both men, in fact. Hugh, except for his habit of disappearing off for a smoke at intervals, is entertaining and easy going. He tells terrible jokes that make both of us shake our heads and he definitely gets the best of both worlds, I reckon: he can talk to us both simultaneously. The two men sign casually and constantly and at one point go into a mock fight for no reason I'm privy to, tussling as we walk under the floodlit trees.

I wonder if they're talking about me.

While the rest of the world is cramming into restaurants we settle into a bar in the canal quarter and relax, first over mugs of hot chocolate and then over more serious drinks. Alcohol takes the last tension out of me. Quite suddenly I find I'm really, *really* enjoying this—in a way that is not at all innocent: having two men all to myself, both of them cute and both of them clearly into me, even if only in a light-hearted way. It makes me feel giddy. Hugh wears a tight T-shirt over wiry muscles and by now I'm wondering what he'd look like undressed, too. The hours melt away unnoticed like the ice in my drinks.

Let's go to a club, Bryn suggests as the last day of the year approaches its end. He knows the route; he's researched everything meticulously online. I'm privately surprised that he's able to appreciate the music, but it turns out he can feel the beat bodily and we dance the New Year in together crammed onto the floor with a hundred others, arms aloft, showered with streamers and shaving foam, before we collapse onto a couch in a corner. And I note with envy how even under the loudest of music the two guys can carry on talking, whereas I have to touch my lips to Hugh's ear just to tell him what I want to drink.

While Hugh is at the bar I try to get Bryn to teach me signs for random objects around me, and he shows me how to finger-spell my name. He doesn't finger-spell to indicate Hugh; the two of them have special name-signs, like signatures. It's around this point that I notice a button on my blouse is undone, but I don't bother to refasten it. I think Bryn notices too, as I flash my hands around in front of my breasts. When I put my fingers delicately on the inside of his thigh and ask for the sign for *leg*, he jolts like I've given him an electric shock and shifts his hips. I laugh and slide my fingers up the fabric toward the juncture of his crotch, a little nervous. That's when he cups my neck and leans in to kiss me, and I feel the electric charge flow from him to me.

Online, this man has fucked me, sodomised me, come in my mouth and all over my tits, tied me up and spanked my ass and made me beg for his cock. But none of it seems as intimate as that warm, exploratory kiss. Inside me, barriers crumble and dissolve into a hot surge of arousal.

Then I feel the clunk of the glasses being set on the table at my thigh, and I look up to see that Hugh has returned triumphant from his mission. He settles back into his chair, eyebrows raised, with a smirking, pointed stare at us. That's when I suddenly get my hearing back: the noise level in the club drops as the DJ switches to a slow ballad—what we used to call a smooching song, back at school. The crowd on the dance-floor breaks up into couples clasping each other.

Bryn sees the change. He points toward the dancers, his brows lifting in an invitation. When I nod, he leads the way. Of course, I could follow round his side of the table, but I choose to go via Hugh's side, almost having to straddle his spread knees. It's not the alcohol at work in me, I swear; I've been very careful. It's the flattery of their double attention that's buoying me up, making me reckless. Bending from the waist, I brush my lips against his cheek. Even I can't tell if it's a tease or an apology.

Then I follow Bryn out onto the dance-floor and slip into his embrace. Oh God, it's been far too long since a bloke last held me. His warmth and his physicality—the pressure of his arms about my waist and back, the toasty aroma of his skin, the press of his hard torso against my soft breasts—they make me lightheaded. As I relax against him the room seems to spin away. I don't register the music any more, just the throb of the slow beat through his body and mine. I nestle my face against his shirt and rub my cheek on the cotton. His arms tighten a little, drawing me closer, and I don't resist. I love the feel of his long firm body and the way my own yields against it. I love the gentle nudge of his pelvis and his thighs against mine and the way my hips tip in instinctive response. He lifts a hand to the small of my back and begins to rub the muscles up the spine. I can feel locks opening inside me, doors being thrown wide, heat running from chamber to chamber like sunlight flooding into hidden rooms. It's the turn of the year and my body is eagerly welcoming the new.

He was right; what he told me. I don't want to be alone tonight.

The music track doesn't last nearly long enough; I'm still familiarising myself with the contours of his torso when the beat changes and I lift my head. But I'm pleased to find that the new song is just as slow and sensual. I'm happy to settle in for another few minutes in his arms.

At that moment a hand falls lightly on my shoulder. 'Excuse me.'

It's Hugh of course, teasingly formal as he draws me away to take his turn with me, like we're participants at some old-time tea-dance. I don't need BSL to interpret the gesture that Bryn makes in response, but there's no actual antagonism in his exasperation, thank God. He can see the humorous side even as his hands protest.

'Hey,' I say, chiding them both, and I take Hugh's arms and wrap myself in them with my back to his chest, reaching out for Bryn again myself. There are grins of surprise and amusement, and I suppose we're all a little self-conscious for a moment, but nobody else nearby seems to take any notice of me being clasped by both men. Swaying gently, I shut my eyes and let their twin embrace float me away into a warm dark dream. The brush of two bodies, the pressure of their hands, the touch of Hugh's lips in my hair as he inhales my scent— I feel like I'm melting softly between them, like chocolate. Oh, I think: I could do this all night.

Memory, like a dropped bottle, shatters inside me. My eyes flash open as the song ends, and with an apologetic squeak I extricate myself from both their arms and hurry back to our table. Necking my orange juice I gather up my knapsack and coat from under the couch.

'What's wrong?' Hugh demands. They're both hovering behind me, staring.

'I'm really sorry! I've got to head back to the station or I'm going to miss the last train tonight. I'm really sorry—I just forgot.' I squeeze both their arms in turn. 'I was having such a great time!'

'We'll walk you there,' Hugh says. He and Bryn are signalling frantically at each other as we leave the club, and I get the impression that there's a heated discussion going on, but it's all over my head and I shrug it off. Outside the air is crisp and smells faintly of gunpowder from the midnight fireworks. The streets are full of underdressed people making their way from club to club. The chill air bites at my legs too; I shed my patterned winter tights when we reached the bar and now there's nothing but bare skin between the tops of my boots and the bottom of my short skirt. I figure I'll manage.

As I get myself sorted I realise I've got a few more minutes than I was counting on; my printout with the train time says ten past, not ten to. We all relax a bit then. Bryn holds his arm out and I link mine in his, pleased. We walk through the streets, taking turns down quieter roads to avoid the crushes outside more popular venues, and when we get to a pedestrian bridge over a canal I pause to look down into the water, charmed by the glints of reflected light.

Hugh instantly takes the opportunity to light a fresh cigarette.

Turning to put my back to the handrail, I look at Bryn with a faint smile. Wordlessly, like a man in a dream, he moves in to kiss me again, shielding me from the night air with his body. One hand slips under my open coat to clasp the small of my back and I arch into the lean of his torso, flowing against him. My thighs feel liquid, without resistance, and he feels more solid by the second. His mouth explores mine with a growing hunger; I'd like him to eat me up. He's half-hard already. When I moan into his mouth he feels the vibration, and I know that by the immediate flex of his erection and the tensing shift of his muscles. A hand moves up to cup my breast and a thumb drifts over my right nipple, already stiff from the chill, flicking it softly and revelling in its fullness.

Oh God, that touch sends electric messages chasing through every part of my body, lighting up my clit. I feel the tracks of my nerves flaring like strings of LEDs under my skin. I can't help squirming against him, and I don't want to help it. I'm wildly turned on; I have been all evening. My pussy aches, wanting him to full it, and the cold outside is more than balanced by the heat burning inside me.

We part, gasping a little, and experiment with smaller, biting kisses. I wrap my arms about his neck and ruffle that mown turf at the back of his scalp, wondering how soft that velvet would feel between my thighs. Bryn stoops to nibble at my ear and kiss my neck, and through his careful gentleness I can feel his breath coming hard and shallow. The hand on my breast deserts its station to clasp my bum-cheek, squeezing me through my skirt.

Stretching my throat for him, I tilt my head and let my gaze fall on Hugh. He's leaning forward on the railing a few feet away, smoking his roll-up idly and watching us, his expression inscrutable. Lifting my right thigh around Bryn's in an unambiguous invitation for him to nestle closer, I feel my skirt ride up, gifting Hugh with a new view. His attention zeroes in and his lips tighten. My eyelids droop and flutter as Bryn shifts his grip on my bottom, reaching round and down for the hem of my skirt, sliding it up to explore the full swell. My skin thrills to his big warm hand. He's looking for the edge of my panties, I realise, but it takes him a while to find it because I'm wearing a thong; a wispy, lacy little thing picked deliberately for our meeting: might-get-lucky knickers, fuck-me panties. When he tucks a thumb under the elasticated lace at my hip I gasp involuntarily, knowing he's crossing a boundary.

That's when Bryn's hand makes its irrevocable move to the front, under my rucked-up skirt, his fingertips delicate on the hidden fabric; tickling my pussy, teasing the barely-concealed nub of my clit, tugging the silky gusset aside. Hugh has forgotten to inhale and his cigarette trembles in his fingers. I'm past resistance now, if I ever was capable of it. I don't care we're on a public footbridge and that there are people walking past every few minutes. I don't care what a slut I must look. I just want Bryn to touch me more. I just want to welcome his fingers into my wetness and I'm so grateful for their slick caress on my swollen clit that when it finally happens I whimper out loud.

Bryn lifts his head from my throat and looks at me searchingly. Withdrawing his hands, he lifts them to sign; I grab his hips in frustration and pull his pelvis harder in to me, grinding my bereft mound against him.

'He wants to know if you mind me watching,' Hugh asks, his voice all woolly and hoarse.

I kiss Bryn softly, eagerly, and shake my head. 'Not in the least.'

Hands dance again. I want them to dance on my breasts, in my wet slot.

'He wants to know if you'd like me to touch you too.'

I swallow, my throat suddenly dry, my heart pounding. 'I'd like that very much,' I whisper.

Quietly, Hugh flicks his cigarette into the canal and moves in. Two bodies shield me from the casual glances of pedestrians—and that's a good job, because what they're doing to me could get us all arrested. Two bodies press against mine, warm and slightly clumsy in their eagerness. Two mouths, hot and hungry. I kiss them both in turn, tasting beer on Bryn and smoke on Hugh. Their masculine scent and focus and strength wrap around me. I've never done this before and it's breathtaking. Hands glide over me, and I'm so dizzy I can't think whose is going where. Two on my breasts; unbuttoning my blouse, pulling down the stretchy cotton, stroking my exposed tits, pinching my nipples, kneading the swells of flesh. One between my thighs, fingers sliding inside me, thumb strumming my clit. One—ah, that's Hugh—reaching round behind my ass, competing with the other hand for access to my cunt, lubing itself in my juices and teasing a wicked digit into the tight pucker of my anus. God, those hands: irresistible and overwhelming. They hold me inside and out. My mind breaks into fragments only capable of sensation. I'm lifted, soaring; though my feet never leave the ground it's like those hands are lofting me up into the sky. I'm their kite and their handpuppet and their toy.

Fuck. Hugh's going in my ass. In my ass, in public.

It's terrifying.

It's wonderful.

In moments I'm coming all over their hands, writhing and clenching and gasping, my nails gouging their shoulders. I nearly collapse. They hold me safe as they draw me down from the skies, back into their arms. I'm giggling helplessly, I realise. God, how undignified. Both men nuzzle in to me for a kiss. I snake my hands down to their groins and find two solid erections imprisoned there, straining against the cloth.

'Outside pocket,' I gasp, finally capable of stringing words together. 'My knapsack.'

Hugh reaches over my shoulder and gropes about until he retrieves what I'm talking about: a box of condoms. He shows it to Bryn, who nods. I rub the twin ridges of their cocks, bruising my hands on the denim.

I'm running wet, and not yet sated.

So, like gentlemen, they offer me their arms and walk

me, tucked between them, from the exposed bridge into the network of streets on the other side of the canal. In a few minutes they find a shadowed industrial doorway. Zips purr. My knapsack is flung on the floor. Hugh embraces me from behind and sets his back to the door; Bryn faces me. It's just like when we danced together, except this time Hugh has his hands full of my tits and this time Bryn is pressing me back up against his friend's torso and lifting me and holding my legs. And this time they've both got their cocks out and Bryn is sliding his into me, filling all my need, and Hugh's is rubbing up the crack of my ass, slapping hot against my cold cheeks, and I'm sandwiched between them and sobbing encouragement as Bryn fucks me and Hugh mauls my nipples. It's incredibly uncomfortable and I come like a string of exploding firecrackers in celebration of the New Year.

There's nothing in the world like having two guys at once, no words to describe the sensation of being possessed, of being both more and less than myself, of being pure sex for them.

The moment Bryn lets me down, Hugh pushes me forward against his friend, bending me from the hips and lifting my skirt to plant his cock deep in my hole. I crush my face against Bryn's chest as I get shafted quick and hard, and when Hugh comes he swears like a Catholic.

He clears his throat as we straighten ourselves up and Bryn wraps me in a hug. 'I think you've missed your train, Ellie.'

'Oh well,' I sigh beatifically. 'Worth it.'

'Well...'

I'm aware that he's signing, and that Bryn is nodding.

'We've got a twin room at the hotel. If you like. We'll have to smuggle you into the breakfast sitting, mind.'

I grin at them both. 'But if I go to your room you guys might take advantage of me. Over and over again.'

Hugh twines his hand in my hair and kisses me roughly. 'Oh yes,' he promises. 'All fucking night.'

***

Actually, none of us make it to breakfast. We're so busy screwing that we don't even leave the hotel room until sunset the next day.

***

Back home and online again, I find Bryn is already there and waiting for me.

> *Hello Ellie.*

> *Hi there.* I add a smiley. *'What are you up to?*

> *Just some scripting. How are you doing? Are you OK?*

> *Oh, more than OK.*

> *I want to tell you I had just the greatest time. What about you?*

> *It was wild,* I type, unable to stop grinning. *Unreal.*

ABOUT
THE AUTHORS

Annabeth Leong

Annabeth Leong is frequently confused about her sexuality but enjoys searching for answers.

Her work appears in dozens of anthologies, including the 20th anniversary edition of Best Lesbian Erotica and Heiresses of Russ 2015: the Year's Best Lesbian Speculative Fiction.

She is the author of Untouched: A Sensory Voyage of Voyeurism and Discovery, and the editor of MakerSex: Erotic Stories of Geeks, Hackers, and DIY Projects.

Dale Cameron Lowry

Dale Cameron Lowry lives in the Upper Midwest with a partner and three cats, one of whom enjoys eating dish towels, quilts, and wool socks. It's up to you to guess whether the fabric eater is one of the cats or the partner. When not busy mending items destroyed by the aforementioned fabric eater, Dale is a writer and editor of queer romance and speculative fiction.

Previous careers include sign language linguist, grocery store clerk, journalist, gardener, and camp counselor—not necessarily in that order.

As for favorite time-wasters, high on the list are Tumblr, studying anatomy, getting annoyed at Duolingo, and reading fairy tales.

Sienna Saint-Cyr

Sienna Saint-Cyr once wrote vanilla, mainstream fiction. For years, she suppressed her deep need to write about sex, BDSM, and what true consent means, but putting that naughty boy in a dress, pulling that cute blonde's hair, or being cuffed to a cross was so much more... satisfying. In fiction, of course. Along with writing erotica and romance, Sienna speaks at conventions, workshops, and for private gatherings on such sex-positive topics as a healthy body image, using sexuality to promote healing, and navigating diverse or non-traditional relationships. She writes for sites like fuck.com, fetish.com, and kinkabuse.com.

Leandra Vane

Leandra Vane is a sexuality writer and speaker. Her work tackles concepts in body identity, disability, relationship styles, and kink. She writes a book review and sexuality blog entitled The Unlaced Librarian.

Anna Sky

Anna Sky lives in West Yorkshire with her partner Stephen, and their unruly hound. Having been an avid reader of erotica for years, she started writing in 2012, and a whole world of naughty words and possibilities opened up. She's been published by Peaches Press, House of Erotica, For Books' Sake, Loveslave and more. One of her own anthologies, Naughty Shorts, has even been quoted in a PhD thesis for short-story form.

She regularly attends readings and erotica events in the UK but can also be found behind the dim light of her filthy Kindle late into the night, seeing what naughty words her fellow authors have come up with. Apart from that she's (in no particular order) a geek, red wine drinker, poi hurler, Firefly fan, has a very dirty laugh and loves to perform research for her stories!

Janine Ashbless

Janine Ashbless lives in the north of England. Most of her fiction has paranormal or dark fantasy themes. She has had 11 books of erotica published by Black Lace, Samhain and others. Her short stories have appeared in many anthologies including 'Best Women's Erotica' (three times) and 'Best Bondage Erotica.' She's currently writing an erotic romance trilogy about fallen angels: the first, 'Cover Him with Darkness', published 2014.

For more information on any of our authors, check out www.SexyLittleAuthors.com

And if you loved this anthology, make our authors' day!

Leave a review!

ABOUT
SEXY LITTLE PAGES

Sexy Little Pages is a sex-positive publishing venture that supports and promotes independent erotica authors and editors. As a society we're ashamed of sex and sexuality but we should celebrate it. Sex is an integral part of life, whether it's fun, filthy, flirtatious, unfulfilling, an escape from reality or something else entirely. Our needs, expectations and fantasies are all different so we aim to publish for everybody and every body, across the whole delicious spectrum of gender, ability, and desires.

Get more erotica at
www.SexyLittlePages.com/books

Or sign up to the mailing list at
www.SexyLittlePages.com/newsletter